DESPITE THE ODDS

Let The Streets Choose

JUHNELL MORGAN

URBAN AINT DEAD PRESENTS

CONTENTS

URBAN AINT DEAD

P.O Box 960780

Riverdale GA., 30296

Cover Design: Angel Bearfield / Dynasty Cover Me

Edited & Interior Design: Bianca Shakur / B. Edits www.editwithb.com

Contact Author at www.juhnellmorgan.com

Contact Publisher at www.urbanaintdead.com

Email: urbanaintdead@gmail.com

Print ISBN: 978-1-7355238-4-2

Ebook ISBN: 978-1-7355238-5-9

URBAN AINT DEAD

Like our page on Facebook Page:

www.facebook.com/urbanaintdead

&

Follow us on Instagram:

@urbanaintdead

SUBMISSION GUIDELINES

Submit the first three chapters of your completed manuscript to urbanaintdead@gmail.com, subject line: Your book's title. The manuscript must be in a .doc file and sent as an attachment. The document should be in Times New Roman, double-spaced and in size 12 font. Also, provide your synopsis and full contact information. If sending multiple submissions, they must each be in a separate email.

Have a story but no way to submit it electronically? You can still submit to URBAN AINT DEAD. Send in the first three chapters, written or typed, of your completed manuscript to:

URBAN AINT DEAD

P.O Box 960780

Riverdale GA., 30296

DO NOT send original manuscript. Must be a duplicate.

Provide your synopsis and a cover letter containing your full contact information

Thanks for considering URBAN AINT DEAD.

I dedicate this book to Alice Schwichtenberg. You were the first person to believe in me with more than words, you put actions behind your words. You were there when no one else was and without you, I don't know where I would be right now. Thank you for everything!

ACKNOWLEDGMENTS

The first person that I would like to thank is Christina. You have been going above and beyond to help me reach my best. You are the reason that I can now say that I am a published author, a dream come true and there will never be enough thanks but my actions will show you!

Some of y'all won't be able to read my books for a while until y'all grow up but to all my nieces and nephews... Dennis, Denesha (grandma), Maurice, Larynique (my baby, keep drawing and using your gift), Lil Larry, Larryonne, Larnell and Larrell! Zacarreeya and Ziggy! Matt Matt!

To the ones that I don't know I still love y'all and I want all of y'all to know that you can do anything that you want in life, nothing can stop you but yourself!

Theola, my love for you is endless! You will always be my world!

Amber, my twin... you proved to me what being strong is, and no matter what you are the best sister that l can have!

Tiny, bro they couldn't beat you so they tried to take you out the way, but this ain't the end of us! We will see them streets again! Free my brother Deshawn Morgan!

Gerell, you gave me someone to look up to, you didn't let the hood define you and you went and made something happen. Keep doing you out there and I will do me in here!

Arneshia Morgan... my Mama! You have shown me that no matter what you do in life you can bounce back and do better. Every time we talk, you give me something to keep me going. From the start, when things were bad, I loved you and I knew that you loved me and today we have what we have out of love and you just so happen to be my Mama!

Amy, I didn't forget about you! Thank you for all the letters and pictures over the years (you know how much I love living life through your eyes), you were my first fan and didn't let me give up on myself even when I wanted to! If these prison walls didn't stop me, then you know you can do whatever you want with your life!

143... to the people that know what that means, then you know that it is directed to you. I know one day you two will come back in my life and I will be here with open arms!

I am building and growing with people in my life so if I missed your name, it's not because you don't deserve it, but in the future, you will have your place!

To all the people that helped bring me down and wanted the worst for me, to all the ones that turned their back on me, I thank y'all because y'all made me want to do better. And while my body is locked up, I'm freer than most of y'all! Someone told me that the best way to make your enemies mad is to be happy and successful. Well, I'm about to make y'all furious!

To everybody, wake up from your dreams and turn them into reality! I did it from behind bars, so you can do it from where you are!

Stay Blessed,

Juhnell Morgan

PART ONE

PROLOGUE

We waited a second before driving down the block fast as hell. The Jeep hopped the curb and before I knew it, everybody was out and kicking the front door open. I got out and caught up with them just as they went through the front door. As I entered, the back door comes flying open and the rest of the guys came running in. We caught the niggas at the table counting my money with the drugs sitting off to the side.

Bull, walked up to one of them and slapped him with the banga before saying, "Nigga, you thought you was gonna get away with this shit. Bitch nigga, ain't shit sweet!"

He turned to me. "This the leader of the crew. I got something special for him. Y'all load this shit up so we can finish this and bounce."

I kept my gun aimed at the nigga closest to me as two of the guys stuffed everything back into the duffle bags that were around the table.

I was the closest one to the front door and I turned as I heard a noise. I saw the shadow before the first person came through the door. I tried to swing my pistol around but it was too late.

Boom! Boom!

I didn't feel the shots hit me, but my legs felt like rubber as I fell. I squeezed the trigger as I went down. The shots only hit the wall, but it was enough to push him back out the door. Shots were going off from everywhere. My ears were ringing. I could no longer feel my arm and couldn't lift my hand to shoot. So, I laid there.

I was once just a mama's boy living a normal life and that was all taken away with my mama falling victim to the hood. First by using drugs then by death from a bullet. Now I sell the very same drug that changed my life and I'm lying in a pool of my own blood as bullets flew around me. Is this how I die? How would things have been if mama was still here?

The last sound that I heard before I passed out was sirens and I wondered if they would make it in time or would I be another statistic, a dead 20-year-old black man.

CHAPTER ONE

"John Thompson, please report to the principal's office."

The class went silent and I looked up to find everyone staring at me. My teacher, a robust black woman in her mid-thirties said okay, made her way to her desk and began writing my pass.

Damn! What they calling me to the office for? I know I ain't did shit wrong. I put my stuff in my book bag and walked to the teacher's desk to get a hall pass, and couldn't help but notice two of my female classmates pointing at me whispering.

She finished writing the pass and handed it to me. "If you don't come back, have a nice day."

"Okay, Ms. Bell."

Exiting the classroom, I made my way up the hall to the front office, racking my brain in thought of anything I could've done wrong, but drew a blank. I knew I had done nothing wrong, but being young and black in Chicago, you weren't innocent until proven guilty. You were guilty until proven innocent.

Ms. Bell was my favorite teacher. She had done so much to keep me out of trouble this year. I didn't want to let her down, and even worse, I didn't want to fail mama. We were all we had and she was counting on me.

I don't know what it was, but before I got to the office I knew it was nothing good. I walked in and handed the pass to the secretary, an older black woman with glasses, looking like someone's strict auntie. She looked at it above the rim of her glasses, shifted her eyes back to me and told me to go straight into Mr. Thomas' office. He was the school principal, ironically the only white one in our school district. I headed to the back and walked into his office to find him strokin' his thick mustache behind his mahogany desk. In front of him in one of the two chairs on the opposite side was a white woman that I didn't know.

"Oh, here's John now. How are you doing today?" Mr. Thomas gestured towards the empty seat.

I made my way over and sat next to the white lady, taking note of the gleam on Mr. Thomas's bald head from the bright lights above us. "I'm not in trouble, am I, Mr. Thomas?"

"No, no. Umm. This is Ms. Long. I was just telling her about how I've only heard good things about you even before you started school here."

At the mention of her name, Ms. Long smoothed out her burgundy slacks and wisped a strand of her long brown hair behind her ear to reveal her pearl earrings. She had to be at least thirty, but what did she want with me?

I looked at Mr. Thomas for a few seconds, waiting to see if he was going to tell me what this was about and he continued. "I'm going to leave the two of you to talk. If you need anything, I'll be right outside the door."

Mr. Thomas got up, left the room, and as soon as the door closed the lady began. "As you know, I'm Ms. Long. I work for the Illinois Department of Children and Family Service."

"Me and my Mama don't need no family service, so..."

"John, maybe before today that would've been true, but an hour ago my office got a call from the Chicago Police Department and was informed that there was a homicide."

"Man, what do any of that got to do with me!" This lady was starting to piss me off. "Can you get to the point so I can go back to class?"

"John, your mother was killed today in an attempted robbery..." and that was the last thing I heard.

———

What's happening? What's going on? I could hear voices, but all I saw was black. I slowly began to blink my eyes open and found that Ms. Long and I were no longer the only people in the office. She, the school nurse, and Mr. Thomas surrounded me. I looked back at Ms. Long, and when she looked back down at me it hit me. I was filled with rage. "You lyin' bitch!"

I jumped up and tried to swing on Ms. Long, but somebody grabbed me by my shoulders and stopped me short. I tried to shake them off but whoever it was just tightened their grip.

"Let me the fuck go!"

"I won't do that until you calm down." It was Mr. Thomas.

"I'm not tryin' to hear that. This lady lying, saying my mama got killed!"

"I'm sorry John, but she is not lying."

"Get off of me!" I continued to struggle, but it was useless.

"John!"

"Fuck that!" Try as I might, I was powerless to escape his grasp. *Just as powerless as I am to bring mama back.*

That did it. I lost all the fight in me. I realized now my mama was really gone and I'll never see her again. I crumbled to the ground and started crying. They handed me tissues and let me have my time. Moments later I dried my eyes.

"I'm very sorry for your loss. I know it's painful." Ms. Long handed me more tissues. "You might not understand this now, but always remember, tough times don't last but tough people do."

She squatted down and hugged me, holding me the way a mother would, making me cry harder. I had to get it together. It was time to grow up. I stopped crying, wiped my eyes, and decided from this point on no one would see me shed another tear.

———

We pulled up in front of the tan brick apartment building I've been living in for the last eight months, outside of which a small group of drug dealers were posted, making hand over fist plays. The sky was a cold grey, adding to the paleness of the hood. There was no grass, only dirty littered up concrete as far as the eyes could see. As I got out of the car and started walking up the walkway with Ms. Long, I got a sick feeling in my stomach thinking about going inside and it being empty of my mama's presence. It was a shame. This was the last year in the '90s. She almost made it to the new millennium. Born in the '60s, I know she would've liked that.

I must have slowed down because Ms. Long stopped. "Honey, if you want, you can stay in the car and I can get you enough stuff for a few weeks. We'll come back sometime after the funeral to get the rest."

"No, I can do it, now. I'm okay."

The first door didn't need a key so we walked straight in and started up the stairs. We got to the second-floor landing, and there were people about drinking, smoking, shooting dice and talking casually as though today were a regular day and my mama didn't just get killed. Some of them were my mama's so-called friends, yet they acted like they didn't care. They saw me, put their heads down, and turned away. I didn't feel no type of way. I ain't expect nothing less of them.

I took my key out, opened our apartment door and smelled the sweet scent of my mama's perfume. My eyes filled with tears, but I wasn't about to let them fall.

"Do you have any suitcases or bags to pack your stuff in?"

"Yeah, we got some."

"Okay, do you want me to help you with the packing?"

"Naw, I can do it. I'll let you know if I need any help."

"Well, I guess I'll wait out here."

I went to my room so I could get all my stuff together. The first thing I saw was an envelope on my bed with *Papa* written across it. Papa was the nickname that my mama always used, mainly when nobody else was around. I sat on the bed, picked up the envelope, and held it to my nose. Closing my eyes, I inhaled her scent once more, before exhaling and opening the letter to read.

Papa,

I love you more than life itself. I know the last year or so I haven't been at my best and I'm truly sorry for that, but above all things, I'm sorry you saw me doing drugs. It has taken a while to realize that this ain't the life I want to live. I want what's best for us. I am done with the drugs. I'm going to try and get my old job back. I cashed my check and I'm taking twenty dollars out for a bus pass. I'm leaving you the two hundred dollars that's left. I'll be late coming home so fix yourself something to eat or wait and take me out to eat. No matter what happens, remember, I will forever love you! Kisses and Hugs.

Mama

"I love you too, mama."

I sat and reread the letter a few more times before I could put it down. My mama wrote I love you and I'm sorry all over the card and stuck the money inside.

I grabbed my book bag and went to the closet where we kept the shoebox my mama had been saving since she was 18 years old. No matter what, every time she got some money, she put some up. In our old neighborhood, I would cut grass and wash cars to make money and put up. I opened the door and caught sight of myself in the mirror that hung on the back, just inside. I paused and stared at myself. Something was different. I looked like I had aged ten years since I left for school that morning. It wasn't a hair thing, either. A short cut had always been my style. I was still that dark skin kid with a big nose, but my medium build seemed deflated. It made me feel defeated, or maybe me feeling defeated was causing me to look this way. I had to check that shit. Hunching my shoulders back, I held my chin high, took a deep breath and continued to where the shoebox was stashed. When I took the lid off the shoebox, I couldn't believe my eyes. The money I thought would be there was nowhere close to the amount we had saved. I found the slip that said how much should've been in there, close to fifteen G's. But when I counted it, there was only four hundred thirty, leaving me six hundred thirty to start over with. I hurried and put it in my bag. I then found the other bags and packed my stuff. Ms. Long told me to leave my mama's stuff, but I packed up all the books and pictures she had.

"Okay, are you sure you have everything you want?" Ms. Long asked as she put some papers she was writing on back in her briefcase and stood up.

"Pretty much, except maybe the T.V and radio. Can I take them with me?"

"I don't know about that. We'll have to see if the family that takes you in will allow that. They might already have them at their house. If they don't mind, I'll double back and bring them to you."

"Hold up, what do you mean by *the family that takes me in*? I thought you was taking me home with you. Why can't I just stay here?"

"I thought you understood what was happening. Let me clear it up, you're going to a foster home; people who are willing to take minors in that have nowhere else to go. You could stay there for months, years or they might even adopt you and become your new family. I'm a caseworker, I make sure that you're placed in a stable home. You can't live with me, and there are too many reasons why you cannot stay here by yourself, but mainly because you wouldn't have a legal guardian."

"Alright. Can we just go now?"

We carried all the bags to the front door from the bedroom. "Stay here while I take what I can out to the car," she said.

.   .   .

She walked off with the first couple bags and no sooner than she bent the corner did the door to the apartment across the hall open and a man stepped out. "Man, what's up lil homie, you good?"

It was Corn, the tall, light brown skin guy with the short curly 'fro. He had been my neighbor for as long as I could remember, and as always, he maintained his razor lining. He was slim, and though his mustache was thin, his pockets were far from it. Ms. Kelly was his mother, and though she owned the building he was living in, he controlled all the drugs being sold on the block.

"Yeah, I'm cool, Corn."

"Man, I'm sorry to hear about what happened to your ol' G, real talk." He waited but continued when he saw I ain't have nothing to say. "I don't know what they about to do with you but if you ever need anything, my mom lives here, and…" he went in his pocket to get a pen and piece of paper and wrote something, then handed it to me.

"Here's my phone number. Don't lose it. Call whenever. Okay, lil homie?"

"Yeah but…" I didn't get to finish because Ms. Long was back.

"Let me help y'all with some of these heavy bags so Miss Lady ain't got to keep hitting all the stairs."

"I would appreciate that. Thank you."

"They call me Corn, and it ain't no problem."

He picked up all but three bags and gave Ms. Long a smirk.

She turned away and grabbed two of the bags. "John, lock up and bring the last bag down when you're done."

CHAPTER TWO

Ms. Long told me I was going to a suburb called Addison which was like thirty or something minutes away from Chicago. I sat back and thought about how messed up my day has been. I had a lot of questions I knew wouldn't be answered. I wish I knew why someone would want to kill my mama. She never did nothing to nobody. Where is the God she said was always watching over us?

I felt the car slowing down and opened my eyes as we were going down an off-ramp. I looked out the window and thought about how nice it looked. I was used to the city and this was far from that.

"This the place I'm going to be livin'?"

"Yes, this is the town and the house shouldn't be far from here."

"What's up with me goin' to school?"

"I'm not sure right now, but we should have you back in

school in about a week or so. From what I hear they have a real nice high school."

"What about other kids?"

"What do you mean?"

"I'm saying though, is there other kids going to be staying in the house I'm going to?"

"Oh, yes, I think my reports say they have two other children. Here we are, now, so you can meet them for yourself."

I have been looking at how big the houses were since we turned on the street, but I didn't think I would be living in any of them. I was definitely in the suburbs. The lawns were green and manicured, there were white people out and about walking dogs, and there were Audi A2's, Honda HR-V's, and BMW X5's sitting in the driveways. We parked in front of this big ass brick house that looked like something straight out a movie. "This the house I'm staying at?"

"Yes, this is it. Are you ready?"

I really didn't see it as if I had a choice. "Yeah, I guess so."

Before we could get out the car the front door opened and a short lady came out smiling. She looked like a nice person and her smile almost made me want to smile. Almost. She was five-foot-three, and wasn't fat, but wasn't skinny either. A little lighter than me, she was a peanut butter complexion with long shiny hair. Next, a tall dude came out and for a second, I thought he was Scottie Pippen that played for the Bulls, number 33, I think. But the closer he got, I could tell he wasn't.

Still smiling the lady approached us. "How are you doing, young man? I am Mom and..."

I didn't even let her finish. "Whatcha mean? You ain't my Mama, and I'm not calling you that!"

She stopped smiling and looked at me like I was crazy; that's when Ms. Long started talking.

"Umm, they must have forgot to fill you in on the details of John's situation." The lady shook her head. "Today John's mother was murdered so maybe something else besides mom would be better for a while."

"Oh, I'm sorry to hear that. I'm not trying to take your mom's place, you can call me Mrs. Davis." She looked in the tall dude's direction. "And this is my husband, Mister Davis. Our other children are still at their after-school programs, but they should be home soon. In the meantime, why don't we get your things inside and get you settled in?"

After every bag was out the car and in my new room, Ms. Long left. Mrs. Davis went on to cook dinner, leaving me and Mr. Davis to unpack and have a "little chat" as he put it.

"Now, John, you are excused for that incident earlier, but I swear if you ever raise your god damn voice at me or my wife again, I will beat you so bad, you will wish that you was the one that died, today, instead of your mother. Understood?"

"Yeah, I guess, Mr. Davis."

"It ain't no guessing to it. Try me if you want. Another thing, you will call my wife mom and me dad because that is who we are in this house. Any child that we allow to live here when we don't have to will refer to us as such."

"I didn't ask to come live here."

"But your little bitch ass is here and since you got such a smart mouth, why don't you stand up and see if you a man?"

This dude was big as hell, so what I look like standing up to fight him? I stayed seated. "Man, I'm not no bitch."

"I see you ain't no man either because you still sitting down.

I'll tell you this once, it is only enough room for one man in this house and that's me. So, whenever you feel that you're a man, one of us got to go and it won't be me. Now, get this room together before dinner."

I wanted to cry as soon as he closed the door. I didn't though. I held it in because it wasn't going to make it better. Maybe Ms. Long could find me another place to live; anywhere away from this hell house. This *chat* made me realize that hell is where Ms. Long has just left me- Mr. and Mrs. Davis were the Devil.

For now, I gotta go with the flow, but one way or the other I'm leaving this place.

———

I knew that this day would come, but having a funeral just seems so final that every day I woke up hoping that it was some kind of sick dream. I had been dreading this day, and last night I couldn't sleep at all as I let all my tears fall. I found that not all of them were sad tears, though. I laughed and smiled as I thought about the good times that I had with momma.

Ms. Long brought me an all-black suit and dress shoes to wear to the funeral the day before when she stopped by for a picture of mama. While everyone was sleep and it was still quiet, I got out of bed and took everything to the bathroom to shower. I felt like I was washing away the hurt and pain from losing my momma and when I was done, I got out and got dressed. I didn't like how the suit jacket felt on me, so I took it off and stayed with only the button-up shirt and vest. On the way out of the bathroom, I glanced in the mirror and it felt like the guy looking back wasn't me. He was telling me that I had whatever came my way.

I opened the bathroom door and smelled food being cooked. I really didn't have an appetite, but when I walked past the kitchen, Mrs. Devil heard me and turned around. "Good Morning, John".

I didn't feel that it was a good morning, but I said it back anyways. At least the sun was shining for what it was worth.

"You look real nice in that suit but you're missing the tie."

I shrugged. "I don't know how to put it on."

"Well bring it here and I'll do it." She cut on the kitchen sink faucet and began washing her hands as I left.

I went to my room, grabbed the tie and left the jacket behind. She was waiting in the same spot, drying her hands on a kitchen towel when I returned. She put the tie on me, tucked it into my vest and straightened it out when she was done. I wanted to slap her hand away because it felt like something mama would do and the only reason she was being nice was because Ms. Long was coming to take me to the funeral.

"Now sit down, while I make you a plate."

I wasn't hungry, but I did what she told me to do. She brought a plate with pancakes, bacon, and eggs.

"Thank you." I played with the food more than I ate it, and was halfway done when the doorbell rang.

Knowing that it was Ms. Long, Mrs. Devil said, "Dump the rest of that and grab your coat because it's raining outside."

I was rushing to get out the house so after I cleaned the plate off and put it in the sink, I grabbed my coat and mumbled, "bye" as I walked past Mrs. Devil and hurried up and got in the car with Ms. Long.

"Hi, John. How are you?" She asked as we pulled out of the driveway.

I didn't even bother to face her as I sat looking out the window. "I'm not doing good. I don't like them people. Can you find me somewhere else to live?"

"I know it's hard and it might take some time to get used to, but it'll get better. You're in one of the best homes that I've seen and given your age, there are not many families that will take you in. The only place you'll go after this will be a group home and you'd not like that." She said she really cared, but I could tell she was just saying that to make me feel better.

"Anywhere would be better, but whatever." I wasn't going to waste my time trying to change her mind. I let my thoughts go back to my mama.

It felt weird getting back to Chicago and a thought crossed my mind. I turned to Ms. Long. "Did they find the person that killed my mama?"

"I'm not sure honey, but normally the police would contact my office in case they need to talk to the family. I will let you know if I hear something."

I looked back out the window as I thought to myself why I even bothered. This lady didn't have an answer for nothing. She parked and I got out and away from her so fast I didn't pay attention to anything around me.

"Lil homie, slow down. Where are you going?" The voice was familiar, so I looked back and who I saw made me stop. It was Corn.

He made it to me, asked me what was up and gave me some dap.

"Man, this shit ain't fair. Who gets to take my momma from me? Then I got to live with some dumb ass people who don't even like me. And that lady ain't no help at all." I pointed at Ms. Long.

Processing what I said, Corn nodded slowly before placing his hand on my shoulder. "I feel you. It's fucked up. But nobody else matters but you and your Ol' G, today. I wasn't about to let them bury her like she was nobody, so I paid for everything to look nice. Let's put your mom to rest first and we will talk about the other stuff later."

I nodded and followed him into a white building on the corner. Upfront rested an all-white casket with gold trimming and white and red flowers atop. Just like her name, it was her favorite flower, Jasmine. Behind it was a big picture of my mama that Ms. Long had asked me for. I made a mental note to get it back before returning to the Davis's house.

I made my way to the front and when I was standing in front of the picture it was like I was looking in her eyes for real. Like my head was messing with me because it was like they were telling me to talk to her.

"Mama, why did they have to take you from me? Now, I don't have anybody and everybody is treating me wrong like I did something bad to them. I really just want you to come back. I miss you, Mama." I stood there with my hand on the casket and looked at her picture, wishing that she could say something back. I know that if she was here, she would hug me and tell me that she loved me. "If what you said about your parents watching over you is true then I know you're watching me. I love you, Mama."

I turned around and walked to Corn and Ms. Long who were standing by the first row of chairs. I asked Corn. "What's next?"

"The pastor will come out and pray. You can say a few words about your mom and we will take her to the cemetery where we will bury her. I got her a nice headstone but it'll take some time before it's done."

"I don't want to do all that, can't we just bury her?"

"If that's what you want, then we'll do that. Hold on, real quick." He went and knocked on the door in the back that was behind the casket and when the door opened, he talked to someone inside and then came back to stand beside me. "Alright, let's go."

We walked outside, I got in the car with Ms. Long and Corn got into his car. We pulled in front of the building where three guys in suits wheeled my mama's casket out and put it in the back of the hearse. Then, two of them got in the front seat and pulled off. We followed behind it for only a ten-minute drive, before we turned and drove past a sign that said, "Concordia Cemetery" and made a few turns before we pulled up to four guys wearing brown pants and shirts with the cemetery's name on them.

Ms. Long stayed in the car as the four men pulled the casket out and carried it to the graveside, before setting it down and walking off to the side. Corn walked with me and stood next to me beside the casket.

"Say your goodbyes to her."

"Already did."

He waved the guys back over and one of them did something and the casket lowered into the ground. Finished, we walked off.

"Look, Lil Homie, I gave you my number if shit went bad for you, but I don't want you calling because something isn't going your way. I got you if you really need me. Just give yourself some time to get over losing your moms and if after that you want to come back to the city, I'll come get you. That's my word."

I could only nod to that. He opened the door to Ms. Long's

car and I got in. He closed it and she pulled off. I asked for my picture back, she returned it and for the rest of the ride, we traveled in silence. I dreaded my return to the hell house, but did feel better about one thing: If nothing else, I knew that I had at least one person that gave a fuck about me and wasn't just talking.

CHAPTER THREE

I've been living with Mr. and Mrs. Devil in the hell house for six months now and things have only gotten worse. For the most part, I was getting my ass beat for the littlest shit and treated like a slave. I had met the other two kids that evening when they got home from their after-school activities; a boy named Tyrone, and a girl named April. Neither of them were treated the way I was. Every time I tried to tell Ms. Long, she acted like I was lying because they told her that I was fighting with the neighborhood kids, so her good-for-nothing ass wouldn't move me. I thought about calling Corn a few times, but I wanted some kind of plan put together before I did that. Mentally, my top priority is to pay my foster dad back for all the shit he's been pullin'. I don't know how or when I was going to do it, but I swear on my life he going to get his.

It took them two weeks to get me into school, and that was about the only good thing that happened. It was about ten or so black people, but they all acted like straight white people. I stayed to myself, but all that changed when this mid-height, fade rocking, light skinned guy stepped to me about April.

"What's good with it, homeboy?"

My first thought was he was the same as them other black cats around here, but that changed real quick.

"Shit, what's up?" He couldn't have been no more than 130 pounds.

"Man, ain't April yo sistah?" He said.

"Hell naw, she ain't my people!"

"I'm sayin' though y'all live in the same crib, so shit she gotta be something to you."

"Man, I just told you that she ain't none of my people. I live with them cause my mama got killed."

I knew it was some bullshit to make dude step to me. He wanted to get at April, which was waste of time because she ain't about to get down with her Miss Goody two-shoes ass.

"Man, my bad, homeboy. I ain't know shit was like that. You know what, fuck shorty. They call me, Lil Tone."

From that day on, we were jam-tight, wasn't nothing able to come between us. I was on my way to school and now I was giving a lot of thought about giving Corn a call. I was sick of this shit. Three months had passed. Something had to give. I just need to stack some paper first.

When I got to school, Lil Tone was waiting where the bus drops us off and his first words were music to my ears. "If I start getting money, would you ride with me?"

"What?! Nigga, is that even a question? Hell yeah, I'll ride with you. Just tell me how and I'm down."

"We ain't got the time, now, and I don't want to talk about it in school so you'll need to try to come over to my crib after school."

"Man, you know how that shit is, but I'll try to be there, alright?"

"Yeah homie, do that."

"That's what's up, homie. I'll get at you later, then. I gotta see my math teacher before class starts." I gave him some dap and spun off.

The rest of the day I was trying to figure out how I was going to get out, tonight. The day was going slow as hell. I couldn't get no work done. I had money on my mind.

Finally, the last bell rang and I didn't waste no time getting my shit and getting on the bus. As soon as I got home, I drove on Mama Devil.

"Mama, I'm trying to go over to Lil Tone's house for a little while. Is it cool if I go?"

I hate calling that bitch mama, but when I wanted to do something. I'll call her whatever she wanted to be called.

"I don't know if your dad will approve of that. He wants you to join an after-school program like Tyrone and April."

"It's only three months left in the school year, it's a little late for me to join anything. I don't plan to make this an everyday thing. Can I just go?"

I hope this bitch don't think I'm about to beg her like Tyrone does. My mama told me to never give anybody that kind of satisfaction. If she said no, it is what it is. Real talk.

"If I let you go, then what do you plan to do for me?"

"I don't know, you want me to wash your car or something?"

"No, you're going to do that, anyway. I'm going to let you go and let's just say you owe me one, okay?"

It was just something real devilish about the way she said it with that smile. I didn't like agreeing to owe her and not knowing what it was, but this was important so I went with it.

"You got to be back by seven and I'm not driving you."

"That's cool, I'll just ride my bike. Thank you."

I went to my room and after locking the door I went to the spot where I stashed my money. I didn't know how much I should take; I just knew that it takes money to make money. To be safe I took the whole six-thirty. That should be more than enough for whatever the business was.

———

It was still a little cold for March so the ride over was a bitch, but it had to be done. Lil Tone stayed on the poor side of town where all the gang-bangin' and drug dealing went on. The closer I got, the scenery began to change. I found myself amazed that we went to the same school. The block was lined with row houses. Before long I was at his crib on Michael Lane. He lived in a row house also.

Lil Tone's Mama was sitting on the couch with her forty ounce of Colt 45. I was always taken back by how young she looked. With her caramel complexion, curly sandy hair, and nice body that remained tight, she could easily pass for Lil Tone's big sister. She was the kind of woman a guy's friends see but try not to get caught staring at.

"Hey, how you doin', Mama T?"

"You know me; as long as I got a Colt 45, I'm good. What's up with you?"

"Nothin' much, just doing me. Lil Tone here?"

"Yeah, he's in his room waiting on you so you can go back."

Outside of school, I probably was the only person to hear Lil Tone's real name because only his Mama used it. He'll get mad if she used it around anybody else. The few times I did slip and called him by it, he ain't trip, but it'll get real ugly if somebody else did. I walked into his room and he was laying back listening to WGCI on the radio.

"What's good, homie?"

"Man, what's happenin'? I almost thought shit was dead for today, but I see you got here."

"Yeah, but I'm in that bitch debt now, so this better be good."

"Oh, it is, trust me on that, my nigga. Check it, you know my cuz be sellin' that shit, right?"

"Yeah, I know, but I know you ain't tryin' to get with that."

"Right, but I need some money, so I went to holla at him and he hooked me up with this dude that be fuckin' with the weed."

Lil Tone laid out how he met with the Latino that stayed down the block who had truckloads of weed. We were going to get paid by selling and making deliveries. Once we saved up enough money we could start doing our own thing.

I didn't know shit about selling weed or any other drug for that matter but I can't see myself taking a bunch of risks making somebody else's pockets fat. I ain't got no plans to get caught, but if I do, I want to be caught with my own shit.

"So, how you wanna do it?"

I already had a plan, but I wanted to see if he was on the same thing I was on.

"Shit, if you mean do I want to keep selling for him or do our own thing once we get the money, I want to get our own thing going. I don't even want to sell shit for him but we gotta start somewhere. Ya feel me?"

"Yeah, that's the exact same thing I was thinkin'. I'm only trying to get pounds but that might cost and take a while for us to save up."

"Did you ask him how much we gon' be making or how much we had to have before we can get our own?"

I didn't want to say shit about the money, but I had to because I didn't want to get ahead of myself and get played.

"Naw, I ain't ask him shit 'cause I wanted to holla at you first. He told me to come over whenever we were ready to talk business. If you ready to go, we can slide through there, now."

"Yeah, but when we get there, let me talk to dude first."

"Alright, let's go."

CHAPTER FOUR

Homie's crib was nothing but half a block away; at least that's where he posted up and did his business. He, too, lived under the same conditions as Lil Tone. I guess there really was a hood everywhere. A short, slim, baby faced Mexican with a buzz cut opened the door and looked me up and down. For a Mexican, he was light-skinned; real light, almost looked white.

He gave Lil Tone a quizzical look, and I looked from him to Lil Tone, then back to him.

"He's good. He's with me," Lil Tone said. "This is John. My homie I been tellin' you bout."

He looked back at me, taking me in again before finally stepping back to let us in. As soon as the door closed behind us, he got to talking. "Two things; don't be running around telling your little friends about me or none of my business. Y'all really shouldn't say nothing about y'all business either, but that's on y'all. The second thing is under no circumstances after today do y'all come over here unannounced. This is business. Both of y'all understand and cool with that?"

We both nodded our heads.

"Okay, good now we can get down to business." He walked to the kitchen and we followed close behind. He stood behind a table and we stopped in front of it across from him. He faced us and addressed me. "What's yo name, homie?"

"John."

"Okay, that'll work for now but we going to have to come up with something different for them streets. It's never wise to use yo real name."

"I think I'll stick with my real name cause that's what my mama wanted me to be called, so that's what I'll be called."

He raised his eyebrow at me like I'm crazy or some shit before he started smiling.

"I like that playa, 'cause I said pretty much the same thing a few years ago when I got started, so we think alike. What's yo middle name?"

"Bishop."

"I bet when she gets mad at you or something she use yo whole name. She must of known you was going to be a boss one day."

"That's cool. I'll go by Bishop."

"My middle name is Hector, but I go by Hectic," he said. "Lil Tone, I like this guy."

"That's my homie. I told you he was good people," Lil Tone answered with a smile.

"Y'all good on something to drink? I only got beers."

"Naw, we cool on that, but we lookin' for some weed," I said ready to get down to business.

"To smoke?"

"Naw, to sell."

"Oh, okay," he said after a nervous laugh. "You had me a little spooked 'cause if you smoke it, you can't sell it. You'll never make no money like that. Did Lil Tone let you know what I told him?"

"Yeah, but we want to know how much we gotta have to get a whole pound?"

"I see y'all thinking big. I like that. When y'all get enough money, which shouldn't take long, I'll give y'all the first four pounds for three-fifty each, which is half the price. After that, I'll see if y'all really trying to get money. I won't charge full price, but it'll go up to five-hundred a pound. Think that's fair enough?"

He said three-hundred-fifty dollars and I didn't care what he said after that. I knew we were on, now. I wanted to find out more.

"Yeah, that's more than fair. So, how much can we make off a pound?"

"That really depends, it's a lot of people in this small-town selling weed, so it comes down to who got the best shit. What y'all getting is by far the best, straight grade A green. Y'all got room to play with it, off a zone bag, up twelve dime bags at the most. You times that by sixteen and you making one-thousand-nine-hundred-twenty dollars off a pound. Re-up and y'all got one thousand four hundred twenty dollars to split between y'all."

"Damn, so you sayin' we can make seven-hundred dollars each off a pound of weed?" Lil Tone was smiling from ear to ear.

"And that's selling big bags so you can build yo clientele, but you can make more if yo bags a little smaller."

"So, how much we gon' be makin' working for you?"

"Now that right there is the golden question. What do y'all think will be fair?"

I was two hundred dollars short to get the two pounds but I got that at home. Fuck it. I got to try, if it don't work, I'll just get one right now and come get the other one later.

"What if I gave you six-hunnit now and owe you a hunnit for the two pounds?"

"Lil homie if you got six-hunnit on you, I'll give you the two pounds for that right now and you won't owe me nothing."

I got the money out my book bag and handed it to Lil Tone who was looking like a kid at the candy store. He counted it first, then handed it to Hectic who counted it and sat it on the table.

"What's y'all favorite color?"

"Red."

It was both of our favorite and just about every day we had it on. Hectic nodded his head before he got up and left without saying another word.

"Man, where you get all that money from?"

"We'll talk about it later."

"But I'm saying why didn't..."

"Man, we'll talk about it later!"

We sat there for like ten minutes without saying nothing before Hectic came back with two bags sitting one on the floor, then poured a bunch of bags of weed on the table out the other one.

"Y'all do owe me a hunnit when I think about it."

"For the weed?"

"Naw, for some phones I bought for y'all but since y'all working with me and not for me, it's up to y'all to pay for them."

"Okay, we can do that. I'll give Lil Tone that and he'll get it to you after school tomorrow."

"Naw, just wait til y'all come get more weed. That's thirty-two ounces right there. The main reason I did it by the zone is so you don't have a whole pound sitting open. Start by bagging up one or two zones 'til things pick up, here's some baggies. Use these as y'all mark so people know red bags y'all shit."

I started putting each ounce in my book bag as I counted them. I zipped my bag up and asked what the numbers to the phones were and how did we get in touch with him.

He got another bag and gave us both a box that had the phones.

"If y'all turn the phones on, my number is already programmed in. You can find your own number outside the box. The phones are burnouts so use 'em for business only. When y'all call me don't say shit. If I say, *what*, hang up and come over. If I answer and don't say nothing, hang up and call back in an hour. Y'all got that?"

"Alright, so I guess that's it for now. We'll holla at you later."

"That's it, but y'all be smart and don't get reckless with that shit."

I got nervous as soon as we stepped out the door. I wanted to run back to Lil Tone's crib. I never did nothing against the law and the thought never crossed my mind but I was on my own now. I was too nervous to talk, so we walked back without saying shit. As soon as we got in his room, Lil Tone started right back with the question.

"Where the fuck you get all that money from and why ain't you tell me you had it before we went over there?"

"I had a little money put up. I ain't know if I had enough so I just ain't say shit."

"Okay, but that's too much weed. How the hell we gon' sell all that? That shit gon' take forever and you barely able to get out the crib so I got to do damn near everything."

"I'm gon' do my part homie. I don't care what it takes, we in this shit together so don't trip on that. Real talk though, I got to leave in about an hour so let's bag some of this shit up."

"I hope so."

We had everything going for us and Mr. and Mrs. Devil wasn't going to stop me.

Even though it took some time, me and April got real cool. I didn't look at her in a sisterly way but she was somebody to kick it with around the house. We were the same age and we had all the same teachers so we did homework together. That's what we were finishing when she said something that scared the shit out of me.

"You know that you and Lil Tone's name is ringing all over town, right?"

"What you mean by that?"

"Damn boy, you ain't gotta play dumb with me. I know what's up, *Bishop*."

I looked at her trying to figure out where she was going. I didn't think so, but would she tell our foster parents? I kicked myself for not being more careful. I know if she knows then Tyrone bitch ass knew, too.

"I'm sayin' though, what's your point in telling me that? And don't be calling me that in this house."

"You trippin' like I'm going to tell on you or something. All I'm tryin' to figure out is, what's up?"

"So, you ain't 'bout to tell yo mama or dad?"

"Boy, you crazy. Them people ain't my parents. My mama and

daddy up in the feds after they got popped off last year for being what they called drug lords. I'm surprised you ain't been heard that. That's why a lot of fake hoes be all in my face like we're cool or something."

I might be lucky on that, but it got to be something she want.

"Naw, I ain't never heard that. I always thought that Mr. and Mrs. Devil was yo people. So, what about Tyrone?"

"Can't you tell his soft mama's boy ass their real son? Why do you call them that?"

"What, Mr. and Mrs. Devil?"

"Yeah."

"This house is hell and them people act like the devil towards me. Anyways, do Tyrone know about what I do with Lil Tone?"

"Hell yeah, he know. He and his weird ass white friends be smokin' hella weed. I saw a few of them with y'all red baggies but he knows it's the one thing he can't say nothing about."

"So, I'm good, right?"

"You cool with me. I'm sayin' though, some of my girls want to buy some weed but scared and shit because you live with me and Lil Tone nasty ass always tryin' to feel up on 'em."

I had to laugh because I know my homie be on some straight freaky shit.

"You know my homie like you, right? That's how we met. He wanted me to hook y'all up."

"I don't like niggas that's lighter than me. I like me some chocolate, so he ain't got no chance. All my girls want to get up with you, though."

"Yeah? Shit, tell ole girl, Sasha, I said what's good, then?"

Shorty was a bad little female. She don't be acting all goofy and shit like most of them girls do. She was only 4 foot 8, long hair with gray eyes; no contacts. Her booty for her size was sitting up right. Even though I like my girls a little lighter, I'll settle for her flawless bronze complexion. Aside from her, there was only one other female at school I would fuck with.

April made a face. "She like you, but she ain't gon' holla."

"Why not?"

"What's up with the weed?" She ignored what I asked and went back to talking about selling weed to her girls.

"All they gotta do is come holla and I got 'em. So, let 'em know they cool."

"Alright, I'ma do that first thang when we get to school. I'm 'bout to go watch *Living Single*. Wait for me in the morning before you go to the bus stop."

Putting all her books in her bag, she got up to leave.

I watched her walk halfway to the door. "You still ain't told me why yo friends won't holla."

She stopped and turned around. "The only reason why none of my girls gon' holla at you is because I told them you already got a girl."

"Man, what!?" My face screwed up instantly. "April, you trippin'. I ain't got no girl. I mean I got a few females that I'll holla at to get some head and shit, but that's nothing."

She smiled and pointed at her chest. "I'm yo girl! At least I will be when you stop being scared." Rolling her eyes, she turned and walked the rest of the way to the door, then stopped. "I'll do more than give you head."

With that, she walked out, closing the door behind her. I was at a complete loss for words. Just to hear her say that made me want to do something to her right now, but everybody was home. I sat back thinking about touching every part of her five-foot, 105 pound body. Nothing like Sasha, April was a redbone. She was petite with long brownish red hair that fell past her shoulders like a waterfall. The sexist part about her was her eyes; they were hazel but shaped like she was mixed with Chinese. She was the other female that I could see myself fucking with.

CHAPTER FIVE

"**B**oy, what the fuck is you doing hanging out that window?"

Damn, how did I slip and forget to lock my door? I was getting the money for the five bags I just sold but ol' girl dropped the money and ran as soon as she heard Ms. Devil yelling.

"I wasn't doing nothing but getting a little air, mama."

"Now you want to lie in my face like I just didn't see that little girl run off and like I ain't been seeing all them different girls coming around here a lot lately. Tyrone told me that you're well known throughout the high school. You're one of the most popular kids, but you don't play sports and you ain't even been here a year. Something tells me that you're up to no good. So, what was that girl doing out there?"

Tyrone bitch ass running his damn mouth like he a saint or something and this dude smoke more weed than a little bit. He ain't nothing but a chubby light skin bitch with a fade. I'm fucking him up before I leave.

Thinking of another quick lie, I said, "She just came over to talk. I didn't ask her to come in 'cause I don't like her like that."

"Okay, now what about all the other girls?"

"They be trying to talk to me, too, but they be on some silly stuff and I don't really like white girls."

"Something tells me that you doing something you ain't got no business doing. I ain't got no proof yet, but let me find out. It's only a couple weeks left of school so if you plan to have any fun this summer with all your little friends yo ass better get yo act together."

"Okay, Mama."

Shit, all the proof she needed was in my pocket.

"You almost made me forget what I came down here for. You remember you owe me for letting you go to your friend's house a few months ago, right?"

I knew this day was coming.

"Yeah, I remember. What you want me to do?"

"Be up in my room in about five minutes. I'll let you know."

As soon as she left, I put up the weed I had. I been keeping three ounces at a time because shit was moving like crazy. I climbed out the window to get the money ol' girl dropped. Luckily, the money ain't blow away. I jumped back in the window and waited another minute before going upstairs.

As soon as I stepped into Mrs. Devil's room, I turned back around because she was naked. She must have been changing.

"My bad. I ain't knock. I thought you said five minutes."

"I did say five minutes. Now come in and stop acting scared. Them little girls ain't showed you a pussy or nipple shot?"

I didn't say nothing she started laughing. "Take yo clothes off."

"Naw, I'm cool."

I still had my back turned to her but my dick was rising from the quick glance I got. I know she was just trying to fuck with my head, but I wasn't about to fall for that.

"I am not asking you. I'm telling you to take off your clothes boy and if you want to play games, I wonder what my husband will have to say about you coming into our room when I ain't got my clothes on. So again, take your clothes off."

I didn't see what choice I had. I started taking off my shirts first, testing her. I had two shirts on, So when I got them both off and she ain't say shit, I said, fuck it and just took everything off. My dick was all the way bricked up now as I was standing there in my birthday suit.

After a few seconds, she said, "Now turn around and let me see that little pee-pee." I turned around. "Damn, who yo daddy is? That ain't no pee-pee that I remembered fifteen-year-old boys having. Shit, that's a grown man dick. If my husband knew you was packin' like that, he'd kick you out. You ever had some pussy?"

"Naw, not yet."

Maybe she ain't playing, but if somebody comes home and sees us like this she would make something up and I'll be the one fucked. I laughed to myself thinking how she dissed her husband saying I got a grown man dick.

"Well, after seeing that motherfucka, I think today might be both of our lucky day. Lay down."

I laid back on the bed. I thought I was dreaming as she knelt by my side and grabbed my dick.

"You ever got your dick sucked?"

"Yeah, I got some head a few times."

"Them little girls don't know what they're doing. Let me take care of you and show you how it's supposed to be done."

She went down, taking just the head in her mouth, sucking and running her tongue around the bottom making me feel something I never felt before. She starts licking my dick up and down, leaving my whole dick wet with her spit. Then, she began licking my balls. She looked me in the eyes as she came up. Then going down, taking my whole dick in her mouth. I thought she was going to take my nuts in there, too, but after a short pause, she came back slow, doing the same thing with her tongue around the bottom of my head.

"Damn, that feels good!"

"You like that, huh?"

I was at a loss for words so I just nodded my head. She started picking up the pace and using her hand. I tried my best to last, but the way she was going, it only took a few minutes for me to nut. She didn't stop after I finished. It felt so good it hurt.

"That was a special treat because you shocked me with that big dick, but now it's your turn to please me. And if you do it right, I just might let you get your first piece of pussy. You ready to eat some pussy?"

"I ain't never ate no pussy before, so I ain't going to know what I'm doing, but I'll try."

"I figured that already, but don't worry about it; just do what I tell you and you'll do good."

That's what I did and I was hooked. She had me start by licking right above her opening. Then I started sucking softly on her lips making her moan with pleasure. I was introduced to my new friend, also known as, pearl tongue. I licked it, then I sucked it and I then sucked it and licked it at the same time.

"Oh... oh yeah, that's it right there! Oh, yeah, now put your... oh... tongue in my pussy and use your hand and press down on my clit."

As soon as I did what she said, she grabbed my head and let out a scream like I was killing her.

If I wasn't hooked already, when her juices filled my mouth, I wanted to live right there. The taste was different but better than any candy I ever had. We did that for a while with her teaching me for the most part. After a while, I was doing it on my own. She held my head a little longer than she did the other times on our last round and then she just went limp like she no longer had any power to move. I started my way up to her titties, sucking on her nipples as she let out soft little moans.

She finally got her strength back after a few minutes. She pulled my face up to hers and start kissing and licking her own juices off my face.

She grabbed my dick and asked. "Oh yeah, you ready to fuck now, ain't you?"

She didn't even wait for me to answer. Guiding my dick to her opening, she put the head in but kept holding it. She put her legs around my waist, loosening her grip. My dick slid in slowly until I was all the way in.

I started to go back up but she tightened her leg around me so I couldn't move.

"Hold on. I ain't had nothing this size up in the kitty in a long time, so let me get used to this."

I think I could've nutted without even moving, just from the wetness and heat. Her pussy was squeezin' and sucking my dick. She then started to grind her hips into mine. "Come on, pull it out slow." I did and got to where just the head was in. She pulled me back in using her legs and I pulled out again and slid back in.

"Yeah, just like that. It feel good don't it?"

"Umm huh."

"Come on, baby. Fuck this pussy nice and slow."

As soon as I started going, I just wanted to go and do me but I did like she told me. With every stroke down she was meeting me halfway. I'm sure everybody says it, but this is the best feeling I ever felt without a question.

The feeling and excitement was getting to me so I slowed down for a few seconds with each stroke so I wouldn't nut. I ain't think it was possible, but it started feeling even better.

Another five minutes and I started losing control. Thankfully, she was ready, too, because I wasn't about to be able to stop myself this time.

"Yeah, that's it, go faster now. Oh, yea! Beat this pussy up! Give me all that dick, baby."

I wasn't trying to hold back no more. I was trying to drill through her shit. Every time I go down and our skin smacked, it sounded like I was hitting the water from our sweat and her juices.

"Come on, baby, nut for me! Oh, baby, I'm about to cum!"

Her moaning got me even more excited, she let out a scream right before her pussy tightened around my dick.

"Oh, shit, I'm nuttin', damn!

"Let it go. I feel you nutting inside me. Oh, yeah!"

It felt like everything drained out of me as I nutted. I collapsed on top of her and we laid there catching our breaths for a few minutes before I rolled off her.

She turned towards me. "Boy, you going to have all them little girls trying to kill each other over you, but make sure you save some for me so I won't have to keep you locked in the house."

I nodded.

"Alright, now go take a good shower so we can be cleaned up before they get home."

I grabbed up all my clothes, still in a daze, not really believing what just happened. I got in the shower, thinking we wouldn't do it again for some time but when I came out my thoughts changed.

"I'm going to start coming to pick you up from school so we can have more time together, I got some things to teach you."

It was every day for the last two weeks of school.

CHAPTER SIX

"Man, you ain't gon' believe what the fuck happened last night, homie."

"What's good Lil Tone, what happened?"

I just got to school; it was our last day. I didn't want to come, but I had a few things to take care of with April and Tyrone that I didn't want to do at the house. April been acting real funny towards me the last couple of weeks and I wanted to see what's up with that. Then I wanted to have a few words with Tyrone about running his damn mouth.

"Man, Joe, my moms was putting some shit up in my room and found an ounce of weed."

"Damn man, that's fucked up. I know she was mad. What she say?"

"Yeah, she was mad but only 'cause we hid it from her. When I got home, her and like five of her friends was sittin' there smoking our shit."

"So, you tellin' me yo moms and her buddies smoke weed and we ain't know shit about it?"

"Yeah, pretty much. She said she'll pay us when she gets her next check, but I'll take that out my chop."

Knowing this will play in my favor, I said, "Naw, we gon let her keep that, but she gotta tell her buddies to come holla at us when they want some."

"Alright, I'll tell her you said that when I get home. Ay, maybe you should leave a few bags layin' around to see if them people smoke."

"That'll be the day hell freeze over 'cause if they do, they ain't gon' be trying to buy it. I'll be over there after school so I can holla at y'all about something, but check it, let me spin on April about something real quick and I'll get at you after school."

"I'll holla at you then, homie."

He gave me some dap and went about his way.

I found April at her locker with all her girls, talking about me until they saw me and got quiet.

"What's good with it, ladies. Y'all think I can get a second to holla at April?"

None of them said nothing to me, but told April to get at them later before walking off. Even though they were gone I didn't say shit, just looked at her.

She got a little attitude. "What's up?"

"That's what the fuck I'm tryin' to figure out, so you tell me."

She put her head down, and for a second, I thought she wasn't going to say shit but just when I was about to say something she said, "You ain't got to cuss at me cause I don't know what you talking about."

"I'm talkin' 'bout you actin' all funny and shit the last couple weeks. I thought you was tryin' to be my girl, or was you just playin' kid games so I wouldn't get with none of yo friends? Shit, you can let me know what's real and I'm not gonna fuck with none of yo friends anyways."

"I did like you. I wasn't playing no games. It's just that I'm not on that with you no more."

"Just like that, huh? What the fuck I do to you?"

"I'm not tryin' to talk about it."

"I'm not about to even be around that much longer, so we'll leave it at that."

The first bell rang and I walked off without saying shit else. I pushed that to the back of my mind because I had better shit to think about. I ain't have time to waste, especially on childish games.

We only had a half day of school today so it went by quick. As soon as we were let out me and Lil Tone met up by my locker. It was a few people that came by to get some weed. When we got outside, we headed towards the bus line where everybody was trying to kick it like they didn't have the whole summer. We were on two different bus routes, but his driver was cool and always let me ride with Lil Tone to his crib across town.

We were one of the first ones to get on and went all the way to the back so we ain't have to worry about nobody behind us listening.

"How long can you stay out today?"

"However long I feel like. Shit, I might spend the night."

"Yeah? So, you finally sayin' fuck them people, huh?"

"Pretty much. That's also what I need to holla at you and Mama T about after we finish that business with Hectic. I'm still trying to catch up with Tyrone hoe ass so I can beat the taste outta his loud mouth ass. You know that's gon' bring some problems with his dad, so I might wait a couple days before I go back."

"It's about time somebody touches his bitch ass up. I ain't liked him since the first days of school. What the fuck he do, though?"

"Shit, like two weeks ago, I almost got caught sellin' some weed to this female out the window. I gave Mrs. Devil a bullshit story that she saw right through. She slipped and told me Tyrone told her I was well known by everybody in the school. So now, she thinks I'm on some other shit. His bitch ass probably told her more than that but that's all she said. Real talk, I been wantin' to beat his ass, but now I got a reason. And after this, I bet he gon' learn to keep his mouth closed."

"Dude a fuck boy for that one. How he gonna act like he ain't smokin' more than anybody?"

"What Hectic talkin' about?" I said switching the subject.

"Shit, right now, just said he'll call when he ready for us to come over."

"Alright, that gives us time to talk to yo moms."

———

The bus pulled up to Lil Tone's stop. We got off and walked to his crib. When he opened the door, we were hit with a cloud of weed smoke. We saw a bunch of older females sitting around smoking joints, playing cards and listening to some old school jams.

At first, nobody saw us but when Mama T did she said, "Ayy! Here go my babies right here. We were just talkin' about y'all, we almost outta weed!"

They was all on some high, loud shit while me and Lil Tone just laughed at their asses.

We walked towards the back room and Mama T was right behind us as we walked in.

When she closed the door I said, "So, y'all just havin' a ball, huh?"

"Yeah, and it ain't no thanks to y'all sneaky asses. We could've been smokin' good if y'all ain't hide it, but I'm going to get on you later about that but for now..."

She went down her shirt and pulled some money out of her bra. "Here the money for what we smokin' now. Then the rest for some more."

"Naw, ma keep your money. Bishop said you good as long as you getting' yo friends to keep buyin' from us."

"Shit, what you think this is? I'm not coming out my pocket for shit. I'm chargin' they ass five dollars a joint so we all getting paid but if y'all want to hook mama up when they ain't getting me high, then I'm all for it."

"Alright, we got you Mama T, but check it, I gotta holla at ya later about somethin', so let me know when you're free to talk."

"You can holla now, what's happening?"

"Since the school year over, I'm about to leave that house, but I need somewhere to put my stuff 'til my homie come pick me up. So, I was wonderin' if I can pay you to keep my stuff here for a while?"

"Boy, I'm not even going to ask you no questions right now 'cause I know your situation, but when or if you feel like talkin' about it, just let me know and don't ever insult me with a question like that again. The doors to this house is always open to you. Now, give me some more weed and let me get out y'all way."

She got another ounce and left. We sat down. I told Lil Tone my whole plan, breaking it down from slowly moving everything I wanted to keep over here to getting back up with Corn.

"So, you movin' back to Chicago, now?" He didn't even wait on my answer before he started talking again. "So, you gon' up and leave a nigga just like that, huh? What you forgot what we got goin' on out here or you just don' give a fuck?"

"Damn, where that come from?"

"Same place where this bullshit you tryin' to pull come from. You sho' don't seem to give a fuck about what I'm gon' do with what I got us started with. When you leave, who gon' be here to help me 'cause I'm not gon' be able to do both sides of the town by myself."

He was still talking, but he blew my mind. Not that I give a fuck about what anybody else thought, but I knew for sure Lil Tone would've been cool with me getting out that hell house. He really just flipped the script on me acting like I'm doing something wrong.

"What you ain't got shit to say now, Bishop?"

I blocked out what he was saying and just told him what I was thinking.

"I don't know why you trippin' man. I thought you was gonna be happy for me. I heard all you saying, but you got me fucked up if you gonna make me go through a guilt trip like I'm wrong or something. You like the brotha I never had and if it was a way for me to stay out here, then I would, but it ain't. So I gotta do what's best for me. Real talk, if you can't..."

I was cut off by my phone ringing.

Hectic was ready for us to come over but I just sat there for a minute not saying shit. I didn't know what he was thinking so I waited to see what he wanted to do.

He jumped up, "Man, fuck that shit. Let's go handle this business."

"Let's ride, but remember that I got yo back, homie, no matter what. So don't think that's gonna change for shit."

He nodded his head and gave me some dap before we left the crib. Mama T and her buddies was still doing their thing and it ain't seem like they would be stopping no time soon. I could tell Lil Tone was still salty while we walked down the street. I just hoped he'll at least mask that shit for Hectic because I know he'll catch on. I really ain't in the mood to explain everything again, especially after Lil Tone flipped the script on me.

CHAPTER SEVEN

Hectic was already waiting at the door. "What's up, young hustlers?"

"Shit, just doin' us."

I went and sat down where I always sit and Lil Tone kept walking through the kitchen.

"So, today was the last day of school, huh? Now y'all free to get a lot more money with it being summer, and all the parties and kids running around with nothing to do but smoke a little weed."

"Yeah, that's the same shit I was thinking. I'm hoping we can move another two pounds a week, so all of us gon' be gettin' mo' money, you feel me?"

We were already selling almost four pounds a week—sometimes more. Hectic let us have one of his phones that a few people called pounds for. It's been three months and we been checking a lot of money.

Lil Tone came back from the kitchen and handed Hectic a

beer, then sat down and opened his own can. I ain't never saw him drink and I really wanted to go hit him in his damn mouth because the reason he was doing it was weak; putting our business on front street. I knew Hectic was going to catch on.

"Man, what the fuck goin' on with y'all?" When we ain't say shit, he started yelling. "I ain't got time for no games so tell me what the fuck's up or get the fuck out and forget about this business we are doing!"

I'm not down with what Lil Tone was on so I got up and started walking towards the door but stopped when Lil Tone started talking.

"I ain't got no problem. It's this nigga turning his back on me."

"I don't even want to hear no more if this got to do with a female. Is that what this about?"

I still wasn't about to say shit but Lil tone ain't seem to give a fuck. "And now I see he really don't' give a fuck 'cause he was just about to walk out right now."

Hectic looked to me. "You was really going to walk out, Bishop?"

"Hell yeah, and I still plan to. All I was doin' was tryin' to hear what he had to say. Not that I gotta explain myself, but you was the one that told us to keep this on a business level, so all I'm doin' is respectin' yo wishes."

"You right. I did say that but I didn't know y'all then and really ain't think y'all was really about real money. But that was then, this is now. Let's sit down and get this out the way."

When I sat back down, he turned to Lil Tone. "Now, don't take this as if I'm taking sides but I'm going to keep it real with you and tell you like it is. You tripping and only thinking for yourself. Now, I do agree he should've been told you and I can't make no excuse for him, but you should've saw this coming."

"Even if I did see it, I didn't think he'd do it."

"Well, if abuse has anything to do with it, you just expect him to stay around to keep getting his ass beat?" Hectic looked at me and I looked away. Taking this as confirmation of his suspicions, he continued. "He's come over here a few times fucked up, but I thought it was from fighting other kids. But now that I know, I'm surprised he stayed this long."

I stayed quiet up until now, but I wasn't about to keep letting Hectic talk for me. "What else can I do? You can come up with me if you want," I said to Lil Tone.

"Hell naw, I'm not about to leave my moms, but you can come live with us, though."

They both looked at me like that was going to change something.

"Yo crib will be the first place they come lookin' and I'm not tryin' to get your moms in no shit. If they don't find me in the crib the police be through here all day so I'll get caught anyways. So, why go through that over and over again?"

"Yeah, I get that but we can..."

I had to cut him off because I wasn't about to keep going through 'why nots' and 'what ifs' with him.

"Look man, if there was another way, I thought of it and it ain't goin' to work. Like I told you many times before, you like a brotha to me and unless you say it's good, I won't leave but think about it first and I'll call my homie. Now, let's handle this business so I can catch up with Tyrone bitch ass. So, Hectic, let us get six pounds."

I went in my bag and toss him the 3 G's. He counted it and tossed it on the table.

"Y'all want it bagged up in zones or the whole pound?"

I looked at Lil Tone for an answer because he had to keep it at his crib.

"Shit, you just do half and half, so when we got to bag up a quick ounce, we ain't got to bust the whole pound down and have to worry about baggin' the whole thing up."

"Bet." Hectic said as he went to the back room.

While we waited for Hectic to return, I was side eying Lil Tone. I had put the ball in his court but I know I can't stay living with them people and if he still wanted me to, then obviously he ain't my homie. I just had to wait and see but til then, fuck it.

Hectic came back with two bags and tossed each of us one of them. I opened the one I had and could tell off top that it was six pounds without having to count it. I looked over at Lil Tone who was already looking at me confused. I then looked at Hectic who was sitting there recounting his money.

"Man, what's up with this?"

"You know, that's a little something something for finishing the school year and a little appreciation for good business. I know y'all got shit to do so get on y'all shit, and Bishop, you better not leave without coming to holla at me first."

"I got you and that's a good look on the extra weed."

"Yeah, we appreciate it, Big Homie."

"That ain't nothing as long as y'all keep playing it smart. Remember I told y'all this, next to a down female, every man needs a real friend. It's hard to find but y'all got it so don't lose it over some small shit."

CHAPTER EIGHT

"Ay them white boys is scary as hell and I doubt any one of 'em will try to jump in, but watch they bitch ass anyways. I got this bitch nigga." I could see his tired ass fade from here. I was about to fuck him up.

"Man, you know they ain't on shit, so let's just beat the fuck outta him. You know I got ta' get my piece too."

"Fuck it, let's do it."

We started walking towards them and when they saw us, they got quiet. I stepped in front of Tyrone. We were almost the same height.

"Yo mama told me you told her something about me, you chubby light skin bitch. What's up with that?"

His homies realized this wasn't a social run-in, so they started backing up. Lil Tone stepped up to the side of him, making him start looking around for a way out.

Before he could even begin speaking, Lil Tone hit him, knocking him right into me.

"Bitch, you was about to start lyin' and shit."

As soon as I hit him in his nose, his shit started leaking and got on my clothes. All his friends took off running and like a true bitch Tyrone tried to explain himself and balled up.

"Please, she made me tell her something! I swear I wasn't... please stop man, I wasn't trying to get you in trouble!"

He was trying his best to cover his head but when he did, we started working his body.

"Bitch..." I started stomping him with each word. "You..." Stomp. "Shouldn't..." Stomp. "Have..." Stomp. "Said..." Stomp. "Shit!"

Kick.

I was about to keep going but I saw that his bitch ass wasn't moving and I heard police sirens. I wasn't trying to get caught on the spot, so I spit on him and we took off to Lil Tone's crib. We had to hit a bunch of cuts because the police were all over the main streets. When we got in the crib, Mama T and her friends was still going with even more people than before.

As soon as she saw us, she jumped up. "What the fuck happened? Where did all this blood come from?"

I looked down and saw that the front of our shirts and shoes was covered in blood. She raised my shirt first because more blood was on me.

"Mama T, we cool. This ain't our blood."

"What the hell happened then?"

"Nothing. We just got in a fight with some dude and busted his nose up."

"I hope you ain't lying to me. Y'all go clean up and get rid of them clothes 'cause I'm not about to even try to get that blood out."

Luckily, I kept a few changes of clean clothes there because I'm too big to fit any of Lil Tone's clothes.

After we showered, we ate some sandwiches then we sat and bagged up a pound and a half of weed.

"Man, I'm going back tonight."

"Why you gonna do that when you know dude gon' get on some other shit?"

"I know, but he a bitch just like his son and I'm not about to run from his coward ass, knowing he wouldn't try the shit with nobody his age or size."

"Yeah, I feel you, but if it gets too bad just hit me up before you come over."

"Alright, but walk halfway with me."

We put everything up before we left and Mama T told us to stay out of trouble. We just took our time walking and talking shit about beating the shit out of Tyrone. He walked just about the whole way, but we parted with a dap and me telling him I'll get at him first thing in the morning. When I got to the crib, none of the lights were on. And when I looked in the garage, the cars were gone, so I figured nobody was home. I grabbed a bag of chips and went into my room. I was watching T.V. for about five minutes when April came in my room.

"You know you in trouble, right?"

"I don't know shit. What you talkin' about?"

She looked at me all stupid before she said, "They got Tyrone at the hospital and he fucked up bad. They just called and said he got a concussion, a broken jaw and nose and some bruised ribs."

"I don't give a fuck about dude, so what do any of that got to do with me?"

Now, I know he ain't running his mouth already. I guess I got to do it again and maybe he'll learn to keep his mouth closed.

"You ain't got to play dumb with me, and ain't no point in trying to play dumb later either, 'cause one of his bitch ass friends ran over here and told his mama you jumped on him. That's how she got to the park before they took him to the hospital. The only good thing is that the police don't know you did it."

"Well, his bitch ass had that comin' and if his bitch ass daddy even think about puttin' his hands on me again, when I come back I'm gon' do his bitch ass in."

"When you come back? That's the second time today you said something that made it seem like you planning to leave. Is that what you plan on doing?"

"I don't know what it is to you 'cause last time I checked you told me to leave you alone and I plan to do that. So go find you some business, shorty."

"Boy, it ain't even like that. I'm just not trying to be played."

"Yeah, so what that gotta do with me? I'm not playin' no games so don't try to flip it on me."

"When you know I was trying to get with you and you start fuckin' another bitch, then you playing games. My mama always told me that I'm second to none, so long as you got that bitch then we ain't on nothing."

"I don't know which one of them young hoes told you that shit but even if it was true it ain't like you was givin' me none. Little hoes ain't good for shit but starting shit and suckin' dick."

"I hope you ain't calling me no hoe 'cause I don't even play like that and for your information, nobody got to tell me shit. I'm a female and can tell and for the last couple of weeks you been getting' some pussy."

"Yeah, whatever shorty, but if you must know then, yeah I'm leavin' real soon."

"I'm going with you, then."

"Shorty, what the fuck is wrong with you? One second you talkin' about we ain't on shit, but now you wanna come with me."

"If you leaving, then I ain't got shit to worry about with your other bitch. So, if you leavin', then I'm gone, too."

The way she was talking made it seem like she knew who I was fuckin but it wasn't no way. Every day me and Mrs. Devil fucked we made sure wasn't nobody coming home and I know she ain't say shit.

"Naw, I don't need anything to throw me off. I'm about to go in them streets head first and I know you're going to get in my way with that childish shit."

"John, I swear I won't be like that. My people taught me how to hold my own and I'll be able to help you. Just give me a chance."

I was feeling April, but I didn't know what was next, so I just shook my head. "Shorty just stay here and keep living the good life."

She surprised me by coming to my bed. Straddling me, she kissed me, then stopped and looked me in the eyes. "This won't be good without you. I'd rather go with you and struggle, than stay here."

She started rocking her hips and when I got hard she slid down to her knees and opened my legs.

She kept looking me in the eyes as she undid my pants and reached in, she stroked me before pulling my dick out. She put the head of my dick in her mouth and started sucking. As her spit started dripping down, she wrapped both of her hands around my dick and started stroking.

She tried to take more of my dick into her mouth and started gagging, but she kept trying, pushing her head further down. She didn't know what she was doing, so I grabbed her chin and lifted her mouth off my dick.

"Get naked Shorty, let me get some pussy." I told her as I started sliding my pants the rest of the way down.

"John, is that what it's going to take for you to know that I'm with you? Because if I do this, I'm not just giving you my body. I want us to be real."

I would have just told her anything, but I could tell she meant what she said.

"Shorty, if I say yea, then I don't want to deal with no goofy shit."

She got naked without saying a word and came to lay in the bed with me.

I rolled on top of her and started rubbing her pussy.

I slipped a finger in and she clenched up. "Please go slow, I've never done this before."

Shorty talked that shit about she'll do more than give me head, but her ass was a virgin.

I knew that I had to take it slow like Mrs. Deviil taught me. I spit on my hand and rubbed it on my dick to make it more wet.

April opened her legs wider and I pushed in her. She grabbed onto the upper part of my arms and dug her nails into me. It felt like I was hitting the back of her pussy.

"It hurts, but push and get it over with."

I looked in her eyes and pushed as hard as I could, getting all my dick in her. She screamed so loud and clamped her legs around me.

She held it. "Now you know that I'm by your side forever, Bishop."

We went slow, looking in each other's eyes as we finished together.

We laid in each other's arms talking for a while before she kissed me and got up to dress. "I'm about to go get all my stuff ready to go. I'll be back when I'm done."

She left and I locked my room door and went to the spot where I kept my money hidden. After I went broke paying for the weed and phone, I didn't keep count of how much I put up so I was shocked when I counted over twelve stacks. I really didn't spend much because it would have been noticed and made Mrs. Devil watch me closer.

I didn't take no money out since I paid for the weed and phones. The only money I took out was the odd money if it didn't reach the whole hundred. I put the money back in the box then put that in a plastic bag and climbed out the window. It was a bush right outside my window where I've been stashing the weed I bring over here. I only plan to keep it there for the night just in case I had to up and leave tonight and not be able to take nothing else.

I got back in my room and I packed up all the other stuff that I didn't want to lose, mostly my mama stuff. Finished, I laid back in my bed and just started thinking about all the stuff that my mama used to tell me that I'll need to know when I wouldn't have her to turn to. I started putting together a plan for what I was going to do. In a way, I was trying to stay woke until dude got home so he couldn't just come in and fuck me up while I was sleep, but I must of dozed off because next thing I knew April was waking me up.

"What the hell you doing?"

"Fuck, it look like I dozed off." I sat up and rubbed at my eyes.

"Well, I'm ready to go."

"We ain't about to leave right now, I'll get yo shit outta here, tomorrow."

I was glad it was April that woke me up instead of dude, but now I wish she'd leave me alone.

"So, you going to wait for dude to get back, knowing he going to fuck you up?"

"I'm not scared of dude bitch ass. His day will come."

"John, that ain't the point. Why wait and go through that bullshit if you ain't got to? Then you going to waste your time coming back trying to get revenge!" She snapped at me with her hands on her hips.

I thought about it and it made sense. "Yeah, I guess you're right, but we ain't got no way to move shit tonight."

"I can tell Sasha to take her brother's car and you can have Tone's ma come get us."

"Alright, do that."

I got my phone out and called Lil Tone. I told him the business and when he told Mama T, she said that she's on the way.

When April came back, I told her that Mama T was on the way and she said that Sasha will be here in a few minutes.

"That's what's up. Now, all we gotta do is get everything outside so we can be ready when they get here."

"Well then, let's hurry up."

It took a lot of trips, but we got most of April's stuff out before Sasha got there.

She looked at all the stuff. "Damn, bitch, you ain't say you was moving the house."

"Don't do me, bitch. You know I gotta have the best and a lot of it."

"I see now, but what you want me to do?"

"Y'all just start putting stuff in the car. I'll go get the rest of the stuff."

We got all our stuff in her van and pulled off, passing Mr. and Mrs. Davis at the stop sign.

———

It's been two weeks since we moved out and nothing has happened. I knew that they didn't report that we were gone because when I snuck over there a couple days ago to blow Mrs. Devil's back out, she told me that they were going to soon give Ms. Long notice and report us as runaways. I was only still sneaking over there because I knew she wouldn't turn me in; not like that anyways. She missed our times together as much as I did, and with Mr. Devil at work and Tyrone still in the hospital, it was all good.

Tyrone bitch ass has learned his lesson. He ain't say nothing about what I did when the police questioned him and he never even told his parents.

We were all just kicking it. I was going to call Corn today, but I had to holla at Lil Tone first. So, as soon as we finished playing Three Man Spades, I got up.

"Man, Lil Tone, let's go for a walk so I can holla at you real quick."

"Alright, but let me go take a piss, first. Then, I'll be ready."

I waited until he left the room before I turned and said to

April, "Shorty, I'm about to make that call to get us picked up, but you gotta know we're all in. Ain't no turning back. So, you sure you wanna go?"

"I know what's up and I'm with you all the way. The only thing I want to know is where we are going to be staying, 'cause I'm not down with living in no streets, boy."

"Shorty, we ain't never goin' out like that. My big homie got us and even if he didn't, I got enough money to handle whatever, so don't worry about your pretty self. Let me take care of this."

"Okay, but hurry up. I'm ready to get away from these weird people."

As soon as I walked out of the room, Lil Tone was coming out of the bathroom. He pointed in the room. "What, she ain't comin'?"

"Naw, I need to holla at you on some one-on-one shit."

"Cool, just meet me outside. I gotta holla at my mom and let her know about the business."

I waited at the door for about a minute before he came out.

"You ready?"

I nodded and we walked off.

We went to the gas station down the street where we got some chips and pop. As we walked and ate our chips, we ain't say nothing to each other. I don't know what was on his mind, but I was thinking of the possibility that he'll still be stuck in the same mind frame as before. I thought about the chance Corn's phone number had changed and the fact I haven't called him since I been out here. Now, I might've fucked up doing something without planning. I guess this what my mama meant when she said, "You live and you learn."

I was in deep thought before Lil Tone broke it.

"Man, keep it one hundred. If I was to tell you that I wanted you to stay out here, would you?"

I asked myself the same question every day and him being my homie I had to tell him what it really was.

"Shit, I'll ask you why, first, and if what you say makes sense, then I'll stay. If what you say has no logic, then I'll have to do what's best for myself and now April, too."

"Yeah, I get that and that's kind of the same way I was thinkin', so since I don't got no real reason to ask you stay here. I ain't got no choice but to give you my blessing." He paused for a second. "But, if you don't keep in touch with me, I'm not gon' forget that shit."

"Man, that goes without say. No matter what, I got yo back. Don't trip, just hit me up and I got you. If it's money, to touch a nigga up or just to kick it, nigga, I'll be here."

No other words were needed so I just gave him a brotherly hug before I called Corn.

PART TWO

CHAPTER NINE

3 months later

"Bishop, get up with yo lazy self, they calling you outside for something."

I woke up in bed to find April standing over me in some lil hot pink shorts and a tank top. It was early. I could tell by the morning sunlight coming through the window. I stretched in my boxers. "Damn, shorty. I just went to sleep. What they want?"

"Boy, how am I suppose to know? They calling you."

"Alright, tell 'em I said hold up."

This better be important. I was sleeping good and really ain't feel like doing shit, but this is what I signed up for. The day me and Lil Tone came to an understanding, I called Corn and thankfully he answered. He was surprised to hear from me, and even though he didn't question me when I first called, he did when he came to pick me and April up. Seeing Addison, he was curious as to why I wanted to leave such a nice neighborhood to return to the trenches. When I told him how bad the people treated me at the house, he had no more to say.

A day later, he put us in an apartment, in some roll houses, and soon as we were settled he started giving us bundles of crack; ten packs with twenty-five rocks each. That brought in one thousand two hundred fifty dollars. At first, we had to give him halfback, but then he put this nigga named Blacky out there. That changed things. Both of us making three hundred dollars daily, and an extra twenty-five dollars every other day. That bundle was gone by 5 o'clock most days, and with nothing else to do, Blacky started taking me with him to hit licks where we caught niggas slipping and robbed them of their drugs and money. Before long, I had April out there selling the weed I was still getting from Hectic, and again things changed. Corn pulled up one day and saw a bunch of students from the high school down the street waiting on the block. He told us that he didn't want his block to be a hang out spot, and when I told him about the weed, he pulled me to the side and told me he was going to give me a block. I would have to pay three hundred dollars for each bundle. He told me if I was going to have weed out there, that I would have to pay four hundred dollars, help him with what he needed, plus keep everything on my block going.

In three months, I did everything to build the block up to what is now. Sometimes I had to work the block and there were times I had to stop everything I was doing to handle business. But I was cool with that because nothing was going to stop me from getting my money.

I threw on some jeans and a t-shirt and went to take a piss, runnin' my hand back and forth across my puffballs. I let April talk me into growing my hair out, and I was rockin' these to help my hair grow faster. I got the .38 cal that Corn gave me just in case a nigga wanted to get out his body. I figured since I was going out that I might as well take some work with me so I grabbed a bundle. We stayed in the back row house on Lotus and Washington where Corn controlled the rocks, so we were selling rocks and weed now.

Lotus Street has four slots of brown brick roll houses. There are two different units per roll house and we stay in the last one. Furthest one back off of Washington. Lotus Street is quiet and no one hangs out here, unlike Washington, which was always busy. The alley is where we sell the drugs, hang out, post up, and protect and it's located between Lotus and Pine. Parking is on each side of the alley allowing enough room for traffic to move up and down, but it's full of potholes.

I stepped out and one of the homies, a husky, dark skin guy named Blacky, came up to me. As usual, he was rocking his nappy 1½ inch haircut. Blacky was five-foot-seven, and sported a VL tattoo under the left corner of his eye. Just by seeing the line of fiends in the alley, I knew what was up before he started moving his purple lips.

"Bishop, we burnt up and missing money, what's up?" It was my job to make sure that it was work on the block at all times, so that wasn't something I wanted to hear.

"Damn, I just left two g-bundles out here and they gon' already?"

"Yeah, this bitch slammin' so hard I thought it was check day or somethin'."

I grab the bundle and handed it to him. "What's good with that other money. You got it all?"

He handed me a handful of money. "The count on point and we gon need some more real soon."

"Rolls! Comin' from Central!"

Rolls is the call to let everybody know that the police was comin'. They really don't fuck with us when we in the alley, but we still had to stay on point. Normally, it's one person on security but it's everybody's job to keep their eyes open.

"Let me get in the crib with this money, but when you finish with this line just come knock on the door. Y'all be safe and keep them eyes open."

I went back in the house and saw April sitting on the couch watching T.V.

"You wanna cook me somethin' to eat, real quick?"

"Whatcha want?" She asked before she got up and walked to the kitchen.

"I don't even care. Just do a few eggs and sausage sandwiches or something quick."

"Alright, is everything good out there?"

"Yeah, all they needed was some more work. I saw yo girls doin' their thing out there with the weed. How its lookin' on that?"

"I knew I forgot to tell you something, yesterday. We low. It's probably enough for two days."

"Damn, April, you gotta be on yo business. I told you that Hectic need to know like five days ahead of time so he can have everything set up. You lucky I already plan to go out to holla at Lil Tone. I told him to let Hectic know we need another ten, but we can't be missin' days so when you down to two pounds make sure you let me know right then."

"I'm sorry baby, but why don't you buy more when you go out there so you know we ain't going to run out?"

"'Cause it be up and down on that shit and we don't need it just sittin' around."

We walked into the kitchen and I sat at the table to count

the money. April started getting my food ready. I put all the money in order by the bill, then put a rubber band around it all. I went to the closet where I kept the money and work. Putting the money away, I grabbed six g-bundles for later. If shit keeps moving like it is with the rocks, the work I got left will be gone, soon. To be on the safe side, I'll tell Corn we'll need more by the morning.

When I got back in the kitchen, April was just finishing my sandwich. I took it before she put it on a plate. "What, you ain't eating?"

"Nope."

"What you doin' tonight?"

"Oh, I thought we can hit the mall and grab a few fits and chill for a while. You good with that?"

"I can't do it tonight 'cause I'm going up north to Roger Park with Corn to hit a stain on some clown. Then, we gon' bag some work up after that."

Really, after we hit that stain, Corn said he got this bitch named Amanda that we could bust down, but I can't tell her that.

"Well, I guess I'll have to wait. Let me know when you got the time."

"Naw, why don't you just get Baby D and Mona to go with you and you grab us some fits so we can take pictures sometime next week."

"I guess, but we better get the pictures done this time or we going to fight, boy."

"Damn, you act like it was my fault that the car fucked up when we were about to go, last time."

When we got to the city, Corn taught us how to drive in a steamer but once we got it down, he gave us a little beat up

Baretta that died on us last month. Two weeks ago, I bought a Cutlass from this female whose baby daddy got popped off and needed twelve hundred.

"Oh, and if you wanna fight, I'll beat it up anytime you ready."

To make sure she knew what I was talking about I looked down at her body and stared at her pussy for a second.

"Boy, you know I wasn't talking about that, with your freaky ass. So, get your mind off that!"

"You lucky I got to get some sleep, otherwise I'll beat that thang up right now."

"No, you wouldn't because it's still sore from the other night. So go your sleepy ass to sleep."

"Alright, I'll let you off this time, but check it. I need you to give Blacky a bundle and get the money from him every time he comes to the door. Don't open the door. Just do it through the mail slot and put everything in order and...."

"Okay boy, I know what to do. What time you want me to get you up at?"

"Like four o'clock."

"I got you. Now, go to sleep."

"Last thing, I already took six bundles out for you."

I went in the room and it seemed like the second my head hit the pillow I was out. By the time I woke up, it felt like I slept for some days. Thinking I overslept, I jumped up ready to cuss April out when she came in the room.

"I was about to wake yo ugly ass up so you can eat before you leave. I got you some JJ's Fish."

"What time is it?"

April pointed at the clock. "Look, boy. You still got twenty-five minutes before the time you told me to wake you up." She shifted her weight on her other foot, narrowed her eyes and pursed her lips. "You thought I let you oversleep, didn't you?"

"Whatever. Where the fish at?"

She sucked her teeth. "Mhmm. It's in the kitchen. Why you want it in bed, King John?"

"Yea." I sat on the edge of the bed. "And while you at it, bring me some hot sauce and a cup of Kool-Aid."

"You trying to get fucked up, boy?" She walked out the room, but yelled from the kitchen. "Is Corn coming to pick you up or are you using the car?"

"He's comin' to get me."

"So, I can use the car, then?"

"Yeah, just fill the tank back up."

She came back in and handed me everything I asked for. "I know that, but baby what you think about me getting my own car?"

"You got yo own money, right?" I was pulling my fish out the bag, and dripping it down with hot sauce.

"Yeah."

"Alright, then. Do what you wanna do with it."

"Well, can you help me find one?"

I was trying to eat and wasn't trying to talk about no car, but I ain't want to diss my baby. "Yeah, I'll help. But for now, can you get my fit ready while I eat this?"

"What you wearing?"

"The black Dickie fit and the Air Force ones."

She left me alone and got my clothes ready. After finishing eating, I went into the bathroom to shower and caught my reflection in the mirror. I needed my hair redone. The new growth was blocking my scalp. I had to keep my shit fresh.

I jumped in the shower and was washing up when April walked in.

"I was just about to call you so you can wash my back for me."

It seemed like shorty was there every time I needed something done. I didn't even have to ask her.

"Yeah, I know. I plan to wash something else too."

She was already naked so she stepped right in and dropped to her knees and put dummy in her mouth until it rocked up, then started going to work on it. The magic she was doing with her tongue and the sight of her head bobbing back and forth made me bust real quick. She took me all the way in her mouth as she drained me of all I had. Without a word, she got up, washed my back and left. I washed again before getting out the shower. Drying off, I brushed my teeth and put my boxers and pants on just as April walked back in.

"Corn here waiting on you."

"Tell him to come in and I'll be ready in like five minutes."

"That's what I told him, but he said he'll be waiting in the car and you better hurry up."

"Alright, I'm done now anyways." I put my shoes on and walked out the bathroom. Sliding my shirt on over my head, I grabbed my banga and was about to put it on my waist, but April stopped me.

"Oh, he said not to bring that with you because he got something else for what y'all doing tonight."

"Well, let me bounce but you know how to get at me if you need something. Otherwise, I'll be back when I can."

"Okay baby. I'll holla at you later."

With that, I went to leave, but not before checking the block before I left. I walked out the house on Lotus' side so I could observe each spot without running into Corn, who was more than likely parked in the alley. Seeing that each slot in the roll houses had a line going, I knew shit was still moving like earlier. I found Blacky in the last slot where the females had weed. He was counting the money when I walked up to him.

"What's happening, homie?"

"Man, this shit still going like we giving it away or something. I think we went through like twelve bundles already and it's about to pick up for the night."

"That's what's up. I'm about to ride and I don't know how long my girl gon' be at the crib, but keep comin' like you been doin' and when she leaves I'll tell her to leave you with ten bundles. One of us should be back before that runs out. Every five-hundred dollars just throw it in the mail slot."

"Bet, you know I got you. I only got thirteen-hundred dollars now, but since you goin' in, why don't you just bring another one of them things and I'll give April the other two hundred dollars with the next one."

"Naw, don't worry about it. Keep that shit. It's only two hundred dollars and I was goin' to hit you anyways, so give me what you got and come grab this while I tell April what's up."

"That's what's up, good lookin', homie."

He handed me what he had and we went towards my crib. When we passed Corn's car, I held up one finger, telling him I'll be ready in a minute. He was on the phone and just nodded his head. I use my key to open the door and when I walked in the house ,April was playing *One in a Million* by Aaliyah while she played *Need For Speed* on Play Station. I hit pause so she can hear me.

"Before you leave give Blacky ten of them bundles so he can have enough while we gon', alright?"

"Yeah, I got you. Now, turn my song back on!"

Just to mess with her, I grabbed the bundle and walked out without turning her song back on.

I came out laughing. Blacky asked what I did as I handed him the bundle.

Before I could answer April came outside yelling. "I'm going to fuck you up if you keep playing with my song, Bishop! And don't act like you ain't hear me!"

"Call me before you leave the block or if you run out."

He nodded his head, gave me some dap and went back to his spot.

CHAPTER TEN

I got in the car with Corn who was just hanging the phone up.

"What's good with it, Big Homie?"

"Man, I'm ready to hit this bitch nigga up and show him how much of a bitch he is."

"Who?" I closed the door.

"Some fat fuck named Big Chris on the Northside."

I shrugged. "You know I'm with it but why you want me to keep my banga here if we running in dude crib?"

"Don't even trip on that. I got you another little somethin' to play with."

He backed out the parking spot and drove past the slots and saw how shit was moving.

"I see you got this bitch jukin' hard. How much y'all movin' now?"

"Shit, right now, we at thirteen-thousand-five-hundred

dollars and the day really just startin' up. If it keep like this we'll make close to thirty stacks."

"Yeah? If I knew this spot would do numbers like that I would've been opened it up. Y'all ain't been having no problem or nothing have y'all?"

"Not really. I just got to keep April on point, but we good. What's up with us puttin' some weed over where you at?"

"What my cut gon' be?"

"Whatcha mean?"

"I'm not going to change up on you with the deal we made with this block 'cause you built it to what it is, but if you come over in my spot with somethin' it got to help me somehow. How about this? You can do you. Just give me ten percent of what you make each week. If it gets to movin' we go in together and I'll put it on my other block in Holy City. That way we make more and split the profit three ways."

"Alright, that's cool with me and I'll holla at April to let her know that's goin' be her job."

"How much you payin' for pounds right now?"

"Four-thousand-five-hundred dollars to get ten pounds, but if I start movin' twenty pounds, then I'll pay seven-thousand-dollars for the dub. I got to pay three-hundred dollars to have it dropped off to me."

"Damn, who you fuckin' with that's connected like that? You know what, I'm going to see if I can holla at a few niggas and see what's up. I think we can do somethin' with that. You be smokin' some of that?"

"No, I don't fuck around."

"Well, I smoke a few sacks and that the best regular I had, so I can get some of my hoes to pick it up for free." His phone rang and he talked for a few minutes before he hung up. "That was one of my hoes. She's up with the nigga, now. Says he wants to stay in for the night, so when they finish fuckin', she goin' to order in some food, but really call me. Now we ain't got to kick no doors in."

"You know, I ain't did no shit like this before so I don't know what you want me to do."

I robbed a few niggas on the street with Blacky, but that was just going in they pockets and getting low after we got the money. This was going in a nigga crib. How we going to get him to tell us where the money at because I know he don't plan to search the whole crib.

"This one gon' be easy 'cause we know ain't nobody else gon' be there and this dude a straight bitch nigga, so it's only gon' take a few slaps and he'll let us know where the money and other stuff at. Just do what I do. Hold up, let me call one of the guys and tell him to bring the bangas out."

We pulled up to the crib where me and my mama used to live. Corn called somebody and not even a minute later, a guy came out the building with a bag. Corn let my window down and I grabbed the bag from dude.

Corn pulled off. "Give me the black one and keep the other one for yourself,"

I opened the bag and handed him the black one which he cocked back and put under his thigh.

I looked at the one I had and asked, "What kind is this?"

"That's a baby nine. Cock it back so one can be in the chamber."

I did what I saw him do, but when I did it, the shell popped out.

"Damn! What I do wrong?"

That shit scared the fuck out of me. I thought I fucked it up.

"You ain't do shit. It was one already in the chamber but now you got to find the shell and put it back in the clip."

I looked around 'til I found it on the side of the seat.

"How I do it?"

"Push that little button and the clip will fall out."

I pushed the only thing I saw and nothing happened.

"No, that's the safety. When you see the red dot, that bitch gon' bark when you touch that trigger."

We stopped at a red light and he said, "First thing, never again touch a shell with yo bare hand. That's a quick way to get caught if you got to body a nigga. It should be some baseball gloves in the bag. Put them on, then wipe the shell and gun off with yo shirt. Then I want you to figure out how to put that shell back in."

I did everything he told me and on the first try, I put the shell in the clip.

"Like this, right?" I asked, showing it to Corn.

"Yeah, you gon' learn real quick. Remember about that safety and always hold it with both hands when you shoot. Don't put yo finger on the trigger till you ready to shoot that bitch, otherwise, you accidentally shoot yourself or somebody else."

"Alright."

I tucked the banga in the same spot under my thigh where I saw Corn put his. He put in a 2Pac *All Eyes On Me* tape, cut on *Hail Mary* and turned the volume up. We ain't say shit for the rest of the ride to the Northside. I was nervous, but I ain't want to show it so I let my seat back and closed my eyes. It seemed to be about thirty minutes when the phone rang. Corn listened without saying shit for minutes before he hung up. He just looked my way and nodded his head which I guess meant that everything was ready to go as planned. I was ready for whatever by the time he pulled up in front of a brick house.

By now, the sun had nearly set, but it was still easy to see Big Chris stayed on a nice block despite the park across the street being filled with gang banga's. Not far from where they were posted, a soccer game was going on. A house up the street that has a few folks hanging out front on the porch draws my attention. There was a pit bull on the chain barking in our direction, but they were far enough away that the people weren't paying us no mind.

"Think them extra eyes might be a problem?" I pointed up the street at the house.

Corn waved them off. "I ain't worried 'bout them. This an inside job, so there won't be no noise unless we have to pop his fat ass. But check it, this nigga know my face so you ring the bell just in case he comes to the door. I'm goin' to be off to the side. If the door opens a little bit, then it's ol'girl so just go in, grab her and put the banga to her head. I'll come in and lead you to the room. Just make sure you hold on to shorty."

I nodded. "Alright, I got you."

We got out the car and walked over to Big Chris's dwelling. It was a two-story brick house with a walk-up porch. We ascended the stairs and I waited till Corn got outta view of the door before I rang the bell. When the door opened slowly, I did just as Corn said.

Corn came through the door and put his banga to shorty head. "Shorty, you play games. I'll have my lil homie blow yo brains out. So, shut up and do what I say!"

He turned to me, "If she'll turn on him, she'll turn on me. So, keep yo eyes open."

I nodded my head but grabbed shorty a little tighter. We

start walking up the stairs towards the room where music was playing. Corn walked in first and dude started to say something, but Corn pointed the banga at him, shutting him up quick.

"Yeah, bitch nigga. You thought you can play with my money. Come hide out and think I can't catch up with yo bitch ass!"

"Damn, it's like that, Corn? I paid you all yo money." For a bitch ass nigga, Big Chris had a deep voice. And this nigga was tall and fat as hell. He had to be all of six-foot-six and 300 pounds. Add that to the fact that he was dark-skinned with nappy dreads, and a face full of razor bumps. This was one big, ugly dude. This bitch I was holding definitely wasn't here for his looks. Corn was right, her lil fine ass was not to be trusted.

"Naw, you paid me what you owed me at first but when you made me wait you slowed my money down. You gotta make up for that."

"What you think? I'm some kind of bitch nigga or something? Naw homie, it ain't even that kinda party."

Corn stood there for a second, then start laughing. "Nigga, you got jokes. Lil homie if that nigga move, put that heat to his ass."

I nodded my head and he went straight to the closet, letting him know that I had the situation under control.

I ain't know what he was doing, but after about five minutes he tossed two duffle bags out the closet, then start hitting the wall with something and start throwing more bags out.

Big Chris was watching the closet the whole time before suddenly turning to ol' girl. "Bitch, I swear on my kid's life I'ma to kill you. I know you got something to do with this!"

I didn't see no tears fall, but his eyes were red and his voice sounded like he was about to cry. He had this coming, but I felt bad for shorty because it didn't seem like Corn planned to take her with us.

"Tell dude to shut his cool ass up, lil homie."

"You heard what the fuck he said. Shut the fuck up!"

For the next two minutes, we all just sat there watching bag after bag getting tossed out the closet until Corn came out covered in drywall. He looked at the pile of bags, shaking his head.

"Man, I know you got more money somewhere. I hope you ain't dumb enough to keep it in one spot, then tell a bust down bitch where it's at."

"Corn, I swear you niggas ain't shit," the bitch I was holding said. "How you gon' play me like that?"

"Bitch, it was too easy to get you to tell everything so what makes you think I'm going to trust you? Lil homie take the bags to the car. I'll watch them now."

He tossed me the keys and I grabbed as many bags as I could and took them out. It took me three trips. On the last trip when I got back in the room Corn was beating the shit out of dude with the banga. I sat there and watched for a minute before he saw me and that's when he stopped.

"Bitch nigga, remember bitches will tell it all after getting some good dick."

He turned to ol' girl. "Don't take it personal, baby girl, it's business."

He slapped the shit out of her, I grabbed the last of the bags, and we left.

We rode in silence just about the whole way back to the crib before he said something.

"That nigga use to be like a brotha to me, but he took that shit too far. Not only did he play with my money, but he ain't want to make up for the losses I took for his actions. My life is money. The only thing that's more important is my ol' G. It's a lot of niggas like that but some will kill a nigga for playing with ten dollars. So, I tell you this outta love. Unless you willing to lose your life for it, don't play with no nigga money."

"I got enough money of my own and any money I need, I know how to work for it."

"Oh, yeah, that's another thing. I know you checkin' a lot of bread and barely spending it. I know you got it in one spot just like dude back there did. You see what happened to him?"

"Where else can I put it? I'm not trusting no bitch besides April and the crib ain't big enough to hide it into many spots."

"I got a safe box at three different banks and I keep my money in them. That way nobody but me knows what's in it and without my password and key ain't nobody getting in there. If you want, I can have the ol' G take you tomorrow afternoon."

"Yeah, I'll do that. Who this bitch you talking about I know?"

"Amanda."

"Amanda?"

I couldn't think of no female with that name except some white girls and I don't see how Corn will be fucking with any of them. "What she look like?"

"Man, that lady that took you off that one day."

"Oh, you talking about Ms. Long. That bitch played me the whole time I lived with them people. What, you been fucking her all this time?"

"Hell yeah, shorty a boss freak. She came for the dick that same night and she ready for anything."

"That what's up, 'cause I'm about to shove my dick all down her throat for leaving me at that house."

"Well, she'll be by the crib at ten, so we got some time to split that money up."

"Alright, I told April we were baggin' up, plus we need mo' work anyway, so, I hope you got a little something ready."

"Yeah, you good on that. Don't even trip. Let's run this hoe and get back on business."

And that's what we did. Amanda didn't know who I was because we kept the lights off, but she was a freak, trying to get me to fuck her all night.

CHAPTER ELEVEN

"Man, I need to come yo way and holla at you."

"I thought you was coming another day?"

I was talking to Hectic. I knew he wasn't going to be quick to change the appointment but I wasn't tripping as long as I could holla at him today.

"Yeah, I know, but I need to holla at cha' about somethin' better."

"I gotta go, but if I see your car when I get back, I'll hit you up and let you know the business."

Without saying nothing else he hung up.

I was just about to get up to get the money ready to go when the phone rang again. Thinking it was Hectic, I picked up and ain't say shit; a code we used when it's not a good time for me to come through.

I was getting ready to hang up until Corn said, "What's up, lil homie? That's how you answer the phone now?"

"Naw, my bad, I thought you was somebody else, but what's good homie?"

"Shit, tryin' to see what you on."

"I'm getting ready to go OT about that little business we talked about the other day. Why? What's up?"

"That bitch from that day been buggin' me to get back with you. At first, I told her you wasn't on that, but she thirsty, so I gave her yo number."

"Alright, I'll just spin her dumb ass. Fuck her. Let me get back at you after I handle this business later."

"Bet then, lil homie."

We hung up and I went to get the money I needed to make this move. April been gone all day trying to get her buddies to jump down on the team. Most of their money-hungry asses should want to so they ain't got to keep fucking for a square and a twenty-two ounce of Old English, but if they ain't on shit there's a bunch of shorties in the hood that'll get down.

I put up all the money we had saved up except twenty G's. Seven for the weed, ten for whatever and the other three was so Corn's ol' G could take April around 63rd and State to the car auction on Saturday.

I took ten G's and locked up the crib. I was going to check on the block but changed my mind because I ain't want to be out there with a pocket full of money. I gave Blacky a key to the crib this morning so when he runs out of work, he can go get it and put the money up. He's been cool all this time, so hopefully, he don't' get on no other shit. I jumped in my whip and hit Lil Tone up just to make sure he wasn't on nothing.

"What's good, who this is?"

"What's good with you, homie?"

"I ain't on shit, you still coming?"

"Yeah, that's why I'm calling just to make sure ain't no change in plans."

"Naw, I'm at the crib waitin' on you, so come on over."

"I'm leaving now. I'll holla in a little bit."

"One, homie."

"One."

I turned on the radio and hit the block before getting on the E-way. I waited until now so I wouldn't get caught in no traffic but shit was still a little slow, so it took forty minutes to get there. I got off at the same exit Ms. Long, or now, Amanda took. Sitting at the light made me think about Mr. and Mrs. Davis so I turned on their street. I pulled up to the house and looked at it, thinking back on the era of life that had been my stay there.

I used to think my first day in the house was the worst day, but it was a time when Mr. Davis made me get down and clean the floor with a toothbrush. If he felt like I was slowing down, he would punch me so hard in my side that it would knock the wind out of me. It'd cause me to throw up and then I'd have to start over again. He would stand over me and dare me to stop. I wouldn't. But it wasn't the fear that kept me going. It was the fact that I would be leaving there when the time was right. To keep from crying as I promised myself I wouldn't on the day my mom died, I would find something to smile about in my head and keep doing what he had me do. Not having to deal with that anymore and having bigger things on my plate, I shrugged and let it leave my mind, driving off to deal with the business at hand.

I pulled up in the alley to find Lil Tone sitting on the hood of a car smoking a square. I parked next to him and got out.

"Damn, you smoke squares now homie?"

"Yeah, sometimes, but just a few a day."

"You know where that's going to lead, but do you? I'm sure Mama T already preaching to you, so I won't. What's on yo mind, though?"

"Man, I'm ready to shake this small ass town and come out there with you. What's up?"

"You already know what's up, my nigga. I got you, but what about Mama T? I know you wasn't trying to leave her. What changed?"

"Ain't shit changed. Shit, she the one who pushed me to holla at you."

"Shit, I can set something up right now. So how much time y'all need before y'all gon' be ready?"

"I'm ready today, but moms got a few things to do. So, if it's cool, I'll go back with you tonight."

"Bet it up. I'm trying to holla at Hectic but he had something else to do. So, we got some time to kill. What you wanna do?"

"Oh shit, I almost forgot. He hit me up and told me to tell you just come over whenever you get here or when you ready."

"Alright, let's go holla at him real quick to get this business out the way."

"Hold up. Let me go lock the crib up."

When he left, I locked the car up and hit April up.

"Hello."

"What's good with it, shorty?"

"Nothin'. What you doin'?"

"I'm out in the 'burbs with Lil Tone handlin' some business."

"I thought that wasn't 'til tomorrow. I wanted to go out there and holla at a few of my girls."

"My bad on that, shorty."

Lil Tone came back and we start walking to Hectic's crib.

"But check it out. Lil Tone about to stay in the extra room for a few days 'til we get a crib for him and Mama T."

"Okay, tell his nasty ass I said, hi, too."

I took the phone off my face. "April said to tell yo nasty ass hi."

"What's good, April? Make sure you got a female waiting asshole naked for me, too. Tell her daddy coming home.'"

We start busting up laughing but I knew he wasn't playing.

"You heard what he said, shorty?"

"Yeah, I heard him. I'm gon' see what I can do. These hoes gon' like him anyways just 'cause that's yo boy. So, it shouldn't be shit."

"Alright, I'll hit you up later."

"Okay, love ya."

"Yup."

I turned the phone off because we were at Hectic's crib and that was one of his rules.

"She said she'll see what she can do, but if she can't find you one, I got a few hoes on the team."

Like always, Hectic opened the door before we even had a chance to knock.

"My bad about earlier on the phone. I wasn't trying to play you but somebody was around."

"It ain't shit. I got a little too comfortable on the phones anyways, so that was my fault, but what's good homie?"

"Same ol' shit, ya know?"

"Yeah, but I got a little something different for you."

We all sat down at the kitchen table before I kept going.

"You remember you told me that if I buy twenty, I can get it for three hundred fifty dollars?"

"Yeah, I remember all my business deals. What's up?"

I got the money out my pocket and tossed it on the table.

"I need twenty A.S.A.P."

He picked up the money and took the rubber band off before he set it back down. He started playing with the rubber band before he said, "That's a big jump from what you been doing. So, I got to ask you your plans."

I didn't tell him everything because I learned not to tell the right hand what the left is doing in this business. After I explained what I needed to, I told him, "And this just the start of it. If shit go as planned, we'll be buying big each time."

"Only because I know you ain't never played games, I am going to do this, but here's the deal. You get the same price and all that but you got to come for fifty or better each time and you got to find your own drivers. If that's cool with you, then I'll have the twenty ready before you hit the road again."

"That's good with me. I gotta make a call to get it picked up, so I'll hit you up then, cool?"

"Yeah." He turned to Lil Tone. "So, what happened? You good or not?"

"Shit good. I'm leaving tonight when he leave."

I look from Lil Tone to Hectic, then back to Lil Tone. "Soo y'all already talked about this, huh?"

"Shit, he been over here every day this week and that's all he talked about. I was about to start charging for counseling sessions for all that talking."

We got a good laugh before I turned and ask Lil Tone, "What's up, you was nervous or something? Like I was going to say naw."

He tried to laugh it off but I gave him a look, letting him know I wanted an answer.

"Man, I was trippin' hard, my bad, homie."

"It really ain't shit. I keep telling you that you like a brother to me and that ain't about to change. Truth be told, every time I talked to you, I wanted to ask you to come to the city. I didn't, 'cause you let me know the business on that and I wasn't about to put you in that position."

"There it go, right there. I told him every day that you wanted him out there with you and probably want to ask a million times by now and you see, Lil Tone, he said the same shit I did."

"Alright, y'all win."

CHAPTER TWELVE

It was three in the afternoon and I figured now was as good a time as ever to clear the air with Blacky about my plans for Lil Tone. "Yoo, Blacky, let me holla at you real quick."

It's been almost a week since Lil Tone came out here with me but we ain't been doing shit but riding, shopping and fucking with some hoes. I even got him a ride the day after he got here when we all went to the auction to get April her car. Last night, I let him know that it was time to get back on business. I told Corn to let me know when he needs somebody to run another joint for him, but until then, I'm going to set him up in my spot. I just don't want Blacky to think I just crossed him out.

"What's happenin' nigga?"

"Shit, really. Y'all good out here?"

"Yeah, everything one hundred."

"Ay, check this out. I'm not tryin' to step on yo toes or nothing like that but my homie just moved out here and I got to find a spot to put him on but 'til then, is you cool with doin' shifts with him?"

"On some real shit I love getting' money, but I was gon' let you know this week that I'm only doin' twelve hours, so that's right on time but I want to do six in the morning 'til six at night. My girl wants me to be home at night with her and the kids."

"Alright, that's what's up and I appreciate it homie, real talk. I need you to do a few mo' days though, to show him how shit go. I got a few things in the makin' that I need to stay focused on so I can't do it."

"Don't trip. I got you."

I gave him some dap and was walking to the crib when April pulled up with three other cars tailing her, all full of females. I was expecting them but figured I had a little more time to have shit set up. Tomorrow we were opening five weed spots and I wanted to sit everybody down. I needed two of them to bag up so I ain't have to do it.

When they got out the cars I counted seventeen females. I knew all of their dirty asses except three but if my girl was good with them, then I'm good. I walked up and hugged April and asked, "This all?"

"Yeah, what you need more or something?"

"Naw, naw. This good enough for now, but give me like five minutes before you bring 'em in, alright?"

"Yup."

I ran into the crib and grabbed four pounds out the stash and split them in half and put them around the living room with some baggies. I had to see who can get shit bagged up the quickest so I don't have to worry about not having shit on the block. Just as I put everything in place, April came in.

"You ready now?"

"Yeah, tell 'em to come in, but first match 'em up in pairs on who you think will work the fastest and send 'em in like that."

"It's gon' be an odd one."

"Oh yeah, don't put Baby D with nobody. I want her on a block."

Baby D was a chubby, five-foot-nine chick from around the way with a gap in the top of her two front teeth and a caramel complexion. I had seen her in the trap a few times and liked how she moved. I knew she would be a good fit for the block.

"Okay, I got you."

I ran and got another pound and some baggies so me, April and Baby D can bag some up too.

The first two that came in were two of the new ones. I sized them up first, then said, "Go sit by a pile but don't do nothing yet."

I told every pair the same thing until April came in with Baby D. Once everything was in order, I started the meeting.

"As all y'all better know, I'm Bishop and I know all but three of y'all but we'll get to that later. First thing, raise yo hand if you smoke weed." All but six hands went up. "Okay, that's on y'all but don't mix that with business. How many of y'all go to school?"

The same number of hands went up which was perfect because I can always have somebody on the block.

"Alright, check it. This how shit gon' go. It'll be three of y'all on each block. Two of y'all will bag up, which will be your position, but you'll be paid just the same."

I broke everything down—the main points being that April is in charge and if anybody played with our money, they will get they ass beat. I gave April a chance to say something but she already told them her part.

"Is there any questions?"

Nobody said nothing, so I went to each of them and bagged up a bag so they could see an example.

"Okay, that's how I want all the bags done and we need this done ASAP 'cause we opening up at seven in the mornin'. So, let's go."

April and Baby D already busted the pound down and had the shit going so I decided to go holla at Lil Tone who was still asleep from being out all night. I know he don't like fucking with rocks, but he said he was down for whatever and that's all I was doing right now for the niggas. I walked in the room and some bust down was in there giving him some head.

"Damn nigga, do yo ass stop? Man, hurry up. We got business to handle."

"I'm almost done. Give me a few minutes."

I walked in my room and started putting together the money I had for Corn so I could drop it off later and let him know everything was good for the morning. Lil Tone still wasn't done so I went in again.

"Shorty, get up. You don't know what the fuck you doin'. Man, homie, we got business."

Lil Tone pushed shorty's head off his dick and put his shit up. Shorty got up, rolling her eyes all crazy and shit, so I had to check her real quick.

"Yo ass betta fix yo eyes before I get my girl to fix 'em for you. Shit, she might give you some tips on suckin' dick, lil worthless hoe. Now, get the fuck outta my crib."

She looked at Lil Tone but when she saw him laughing his ass off, she got dressed.

She walked past me and I smacked her hard as hell on her ass.

"Ouch! Don't touch me!" She said running out the crib.

Lil Tone finished laughing saying, "You ain't have to do her like that, but what's up?"

"Money, that's what's up, nigga. You with it?"

"Come on, homie. You know the answer to that already."

"Act like it then, my homie on the block waiting on you so he can show you how everything moves. Let everybody get used to yo face. You gon' be workin' packs for a couple days just to get yo feet wet, then you and Black gon' start doin' twelve-hour shifts. You good with that?"

"What's up with this pack selling shit. I'm not with that."

"Look, you gon' be out there anyway so why not make some money? That's part of the game. You with it?"

"Yeah, I guess that's cool. What you want me to do now?"

"Just go out there. He been waiting on you for a minute now."

"What you on tonight?"

"Man, I don't party every night. I was just doin' that 'cause you came around but now I'm back chasin' paper. I got five weed spots openin' in the morning and that's what we on now, so let's ride."

I needed to get back to helping bag up and really ain't have time to explain everything to him. If he plans to get any money, he better make his own feet move because I ain't about to let shit slow mine down.

I try to push him past the living room but that would've been too much for him to do with women in the vicinity.

"How you doin' Lil Tone?" One of the worker chicks I was familiar with named Mona asked. Her bowlegged, acne chin face ass. She was five-foot-two, yellow bone with long curly hair that she kept in a side ponytail.

"I'm good. What's up with you?"

I swear all thoughts of money left his mind and that's something we'll have to talk about, but for now, I had to keep my money moving. She was thick as hell, but it wasn't that serious.

"Yo! Real talk, y'all can play love connection some other time. You and Mona got stuff to do."

"Alright, homie. I'll holla at you later, shorty."

As soon as he left, I went around and checked everybody's bags and when I got to the two new girls, I knew I found my baggers. They were skinny with oval shaped faces that anyone would consider to be pretty. They had a chocolate complexion with short hair that was gelled down to their heads, and they were identical. Didn't know why but I liked that. It was different and I got the feeling it would be fun to have them around; beneficial, too, if they kept bagging up the product the way they did.

"Y'all did this before, ain't y'all?"

They ain't even look up, just shook their heads and kept working.

"Y'all want the job of doing this all the time?"

"Yeah, but we gotta be able to smoke, though."

"I don't care what y'all do, as long as the work getting' done and y'all ain't stealing. So, we good or what?"

"How much we getting paid?"

"I don't know yet, but as long as y'all work like this y'all get free weed when ya'll here."

"Just don't try to play us, and call us Twins."

"Bet. Everybody else, if you wanna stop, go ahead."

Everybody got up except the Twins and Baby D. When the two other females saw nobody else wanted to stay, they sat back down.

"That's it?" When nobody moved. I said, "Alright, that's on

y'all. Take what you bagged up and split it with yo partner and that's y'all shit. You can do whatever you want with it. I need everybody back here by six o'clock. Make sure you got a car. I'm puttin' gas money up to make sure everybody makes it."

I could tell they wanted to sit back down but I started picking up the extra and putting it in two piles for the ones that were staying.

After they all got their shit and left, I turned to the ones that stayed, "Okay, y'all should make a lot of bags with that so while we bag up for the blocks ya'll bag up that shit and split it four ways for ya'll and the Twins."

I went and popped in C-Murder's new tape, *Bossalinie,* and grabbed the garbage can. I took all the bags that were bagged up and tossed them in, then sat back down, getting to work. With all of us working, by the time the tape popped, we had gone through close to five pounds. It didn't seem like they were ready to quit but I had other stuff to do so I left them to do them.

I wanted to check on Lil Tone because he seemed like he was a kid in a candy store with all this pussy running around. The plans I had for him, I needed him to be focused.

That shit had to wait, though, I had other shit to do. I called Corn to see what he was on.

He answered on the second ring. "Yo, what the business is?"

"Man, you know what it is. I'm waitin' to see how you wanna do this."

"You at the crib?"

"Yeah."

"Alright, I'll hit you up when I get there. Oh, and bring a few sacks with you."

I hung up. Fuck it. I might as well go check the block.

"April, go as long as y'all want, but that should be enough for a couple days. I'm about to go handle some other business. I don't know when I'll be back, so I'll hit you up later."

"Okay, baby, after we finish this we going to grab something to eat."

I walked outside to the alley and just watched as business went on. For the most part, everything was good. I had to talk with Blacky because it wasn't until Corn called and my phone rang that they noticed that I was sitting there watching them. If I was anybody else, they would've been got.

"What's good, Big Homie?" I walked towards the front of the alley as I answered the phone.

"I'm comin' down Washington right now. Meet me on Pine."

He hung up before I could say anything else. I walked up to Lil Tone and Blacky I saw a few of the females was out there and that's why they weren't paying attention to what was happening around them.

"Man, Mona, don't you got somewhere to go?"

"No, I don't, why?"

"Find somewhere besides here. You fuckin' up business."

She and her buddies gave me a funky ass look but walked off.

"Damn, why you cock blockin' like that?" Lil Tone said.

"'Cause y'all out here slippin'. I was just sittin' back there watchin' y'all for damn near five minutes and y'all didn't see shit. Just think if that was the stick-up kid or worse, the boys. I need y'all to stay on point."

Corn was just pulling up so I ran over so he ain't have to park.

I got in and he got right to business.

"I just want to show you the spots we gon' be workin' on and how I want everything to go. Then, it's a few people you got to meet."

"Alright, that's cool. I got everything settled and I ain't got shit else to do tonight, so we got all night."

"Oh, another thing we need to get straight. I need you to stay out the action. You my top man. I can't afford to lose you so all that kickin' it on the block got to stop. Besides pickin' up our bread, have Blacky and yo homie... umm, Lil Tone take care of the other shit and get April to handle the weed thing."

"I'm cool with that, but dude I'm buyin' from ain't..."

"Naw, you handle that. I know how it is with them connects so you keep doin' that and when we start sellin' pounds, you'll do that too. Just be cool on the block."

"Alright, you the boss."

The rest of the night we went through all the blocks and found the best spots to set up where girls can watch the whole block and they ain't have to carry the weed on them all day.

The people we had to talk to were mainly people on the blocks and just to make a few deals. They don't want blocks full of crack heads around their houses. Said as long as we keep them away, they'll watch out for the girls. The other people were niggas that wanted to test what we had to see if they wanted to cop weight.

Everything seemed to be on the right track. We just had to see if it was going to play out like we planned.

CHAPTER THIRTEEN

"Bishop, Mama T wants to talk to you."

"Where she at?"

I was at the crib counting money and putting it in stacks of five G's before April come in.

"She on the phone," she said as she handed it to me.

"How you doin', Mama T? You got settled in the crib yet?"

"I'm okay, baby. You don't know how much I appreciate the apartment, but look, I'm calling 'cause that boy ain't come home in a few days and I was wondering if he stayed over there?"

"Naw, he ain't over here. At least I don't think so, but let me check."

I got up and went to the back room but he wasn't there so I went to the front room where April and the Twins were bagging up.

"April, did Lil Tone come through here last night or this morning?"

"Nope. Just when he was with you. Something wrong?"

"Naw, Mama T just wondering why he ain't come home last night. Ay, Twins, did y'all see him on the block when y'all come in?"

Just like twins, they responded at the same time, "His mannish ass ain't out there."

"Alright, I'll leave y'all alone now."

I got back on the phone with Mama T.

"Look, he ain't over here, but I'm gon' call around. I'm sure he just laid up with some female but when I holla at him, I'll have his ass hit cha' up."

"Okay, baby. I'll talk to you another time and thank you again for the apartment."

I hung up the phone and shook my head because it feels like I'm babysitting this nigga. He supposed to be running the block and that's not possible if he's MIA. I put up the money I had out and grabbed the banga so I can check the block out.

"Where you going?"

"Nowhere, just gotta check out what's goin' on out there."

"Oh, I thought you was going out. I needed you to go to the store but it's alright. I'll go later."

"You sure, because I can do it now."

"Yeah, I got it, but the Twins need some mo' blunts. You can grab some from the square house?"

"Yeah, I got you when I'm done with this business."

We started getting money on the block and had this old man looking out for us, letting us come in his house if the police got, too, hot. He started selling loose cigarettes and blunts, and he had a mini store so we didn't have to leave the block. We called his spot the square house.

I walked outside and saw shit moving like it was suppose to

so I wasn't too mad, but I still ain't see this nigga. I waited until the worker was finished serving a customer before I walked up to him.

"Ay, where Lil Tone at?"

"You just missed him but he been ridin' through every ten minutes with this female."

"Alright, everything good out here with y'all?"

"Yeah, it's just a little slower than usual, but you know how it is."

"Yeah, I know. It'll pick back up."

Another customer walked up so I left him to handle his business and went to the square house.

"What up with it, youngin'?"

"Not much. Just chasin' a dollar. Everything good with you?"

"Yeah. Just trying to earn my retirement check, ya feel me?"

I start laughing because truth be told he making at least five hundred or better a day.

"Shit, you must be plannin' a big retirement with all the money you checkin'."

"They say go big or go home. I don't see no other way, but you ain't come over to kick it with an old man, so what's up?"

"Let me get a box of White Owls."

He reached back in the door and handed me the box of blunts then said, "Man, let people know I'm doing the bootleg thing too and I'll have all the good shit—white, dark and beer, whatever. So, put the word out there for me."

"I got cha'."

I saw Lil Tone ride up so I said, "Check it, I 'preciate the blunts, but I got to go holla at my homie. I'll get at you later."

"You keep yo eyes open youngin' and make sure you puttin' up for yo retirement, too. This shit ain't forever."

"Alright, I'll holla at cha, Pops."

Lil Tone must ain't see me because when he got out the car, he went the other way. "Ay Lil Tone, let me holla at you, bruh."

As soon as he turned around and saw me, he just got the shit face because he knew he fucked up. He walked up and gave me a pound.

"What's poppin', big bruh?"

"Shit, here, what's up with you?"

"You know me, just doing me."

"Yeah, I know and that's the opposite of what I wanted to hear. First, you ain't go to the crib last night or even call yo ol'G so she called me trippin' and when I came out here lookin' for you, I find out you riding around with a bitch."

"I'm sayin', though, what's wrong with that?"

This nigga must be out his rabbit ass mind, standing here like he ain't fucking up.

"Nigga, if you wasn't my brotha you'll be sittin' on yo back pocket right now."

"What the fuck I do?"

"Is you serious, Joe? The point of runnin' the block is being here to make sure everything straight."

"But I'm ridin'..."

"And that shit makes it worse. You ridin' with some bitch that you just met. Now, what if y'all get pulled ova? How you gon' explain the money in yo pocket or if the bitch set you up to get poked? Fuck that, how the fuck you gon' pay me my money?"

"Alright man. I fucked up, my bad."

"I know you fucked up, but it ain't shit. Just don't do it no more, and call yo moms."

"Alright, I'ma do that but let me get rid of ol' girl, first."

He got to walking towards ol' girl car but I ain't plan to sit out here and wait, so I stopped him.

"Ay, how much bread you got?"

He got the money out and counted it.

"Right now, I got thirteen but it should be some more ready right now."

"It's cool. I'll just take what you got now. Bring the rest when you need more work."

I was about to walk away when I saw the look on his face and could tell he had something on his mind.

He put his head down, then said, "Man, just give me some time to get used to this stuff. On my mama, I'm not gonna make too many more mistakes."

I ain't want to seem too bogus, but he got to realize that this is business and ain't shit about to get in the way of mine.

"Man, whatever you do is up to you as long as you don't fuck up my money."

The way he looked told me he was salty, but I just turned to go back in the crib because I wasn't trying to get into it with him, especially out in the open.

"And don't forget to call yo ol' G!"

I walked in the crib, tossed the blunts in the front room for the twins and went back to my room to finish counting.

April came in the room. "What's wrong with you?"

"Ain't shit wrong with me."

"It got to be something. You came in all mad."

"I'm straight now. Leave me the fuck alone so I can finish this shit."

"First off, don't cuss at me. And second, you ain't straight 'cause if you was, you would've realized that you threw the blunts and hit one of the twins in the face. But you know what, I'm going to leave you the fuck alone like you want me to 'til you get your damn mind straight."

She ain't give me time to say shit before she walked out but I had other shit to do and really wasn't trying to hear none of that shit she was talking about anyways. I got the money back out to finish counting it. Everything was moving so fast with the weed, it was like a real job to keep it up and now Corn is ready to open a few more blocks and start selling pounds.

"Fuck!" This is the second time I lost count and had to start over. The shit with Lil Tone and April was distracting me, but mainly April because she ain't do shit wrong. I put the money up again so I wouldn't fuck nothing up, then went to holla at April. I walked in the front room and damn near lost my mind. Sitting right on the couch was April smoking a blunt.

"What the fuck is you doing shorty?"

She took another pull on the blunt and let the smoke out before she said, "What 'cha talking nigga?"

I looked at the twins and they put their heads down.

"Why the fuck y'all let her hit the blunt? Y'all know Goddamn well she don't smoke!"

"They ain't got shit to do with this, John. I'ma do what the fuck I want to do and since you wanted me to leave you alone, why not kick it with the girls?"

"Put the blunt out and let me talk to you in the room."

"How about you just leave me the fuck alone!"

"There you go, acting like a little fuckin' girl, again. I ain't got time to be babysittin' my homie and my girl, so y'all ass need to grow the fuck up!"

"I don't need you babysittin' me. I do what the fuck I want and not even my daddy gonna stop me, so find some business because babysitting ain't it."

This girl really lost her mind but I'm not about to play these games with her.

"Don't trip, you do you. I'm about to go for a ride so call me when you grow up and got them drugs out yo system."

I was about to grab the gun but thought better of it because if somebody got in my way right now, they might get shot. I grabbed the keys and walked out the house. Before I got in the car April came running out the house.

"What?"

"I just wanted to tell you to get some for me, okay?"

"Get some of what?"

"Some pussy."

She busted out laughing and laid out on the ground. I was about to grab her dumb ass up and take her in the crib but the Twins came to help her up so I just got in the car and pulled off.

C-Murder's *Life Or Death* tape was already in. I turned that shit up and drove.

I didn't even know what I was thinking or how long I'd been driving. Let alone where I was. I realized that my phone was vibrating and looked to see I missed fifteen calls.

I turned the radio down and answered, "Yeah?"

"Why the fuck you ain't been answering yo phone?"

"Man, who the fuck is this callin' my phone talkin' crazy?"

"This Twin, boy. April been tryin' to call you for an hour."

It didn't even feel like I was gone for ten minutes so I must've been spaced out for real. I'm surprised I ain't hit shit or get hit.

"Did she get her mind right and stop smokin' that shit?"

"She was good but now she trippin' 'cause you ain't answering yo phone and Bishop, she only smoked some weed. It's not that bad and if it was, why you sell it?"

"I don't know what other people do with their lives and if she wasn't doin' it just to get at me, I'll be cool with it but she was actin' like a kid and y'all know how I feel about that shit. Anyways, put her on the phone."

"Hold up."

After a few seconds, I heard April scream something and I knew I should've hung up then but I decided to hear her out. As she got closer to the phone and I heard the Twins trying to tell her to chill.

"Nigga, where the fuck you at? Why you ain't been answering the damn phone?"

"Shorty, you need to pipe down with all that noise and act like you got some kind of sense."

"I'm not trying to hear none of that, John. Where you at?"

"I don't know..."

"Whatcha mean? Don't do me, boy!"

I could tell she was crying but she was working herself up over nothing.

"I was just driving and got lost in thought. I looked up and didn't know where I was at."

"You a damn liar, but if you going to fuck another hoe, then I might as well go find me a nigga. I know Lil Tone still wants to hit it."

"Shorty, I swear on my mama grave if you ever do or say some shit like..."

I saw the police behind me with their lights on.

"Fuck! You stupid bitch, fuckin' with you the police on my ass now. Fuck!"

"Stop playing like that, baby!"

"Bitch, I'm not playin'."

I was trying to figure out where I was but I never heard of none of these streets.

"Don't pull over. Just try to make it back home."

"I'm lost. How the hell I'm gon' get home? Call Corn, I gotta pull over now."

"I'm sorry, baby!"

CHAPTER FOURTEEN

I hung up, not even trying to hear that shit. I pulled over and turned the car off. The police jumped out with guns up and for the first time I saw that it was the Maywood Police.

"Get your hands up and step out of the car!"

I did what they said.

"Now, back up three steps and get on your knees."

As soon as I did what they told me, one of them bitches tackled and cuffed me up.

"What you got on you?"

"Nothing, man. Why you have to do all this?"

"What's in the car?"

"Ain't shit in the car!"

He pats me down and when he ain't find nothing he asked, "Why you ain't stop when we got behind you? I know you saw the lights."

"I didn't see y'all 'til about a half of a block ago, but before that, I was tryin' to get directions on the phone."

I was nervous because I knew I was going back to them people but hopefully, my plan works out and I get back home tonight.

"You got a license?"

"Nope."

"Who's car is this?"

"My friend's mama's, I think."

"And what this friend's name?"

"I don't know his real name."

"Yeah, I knew you were going to say that. If you don't tell us now if it's something in the car or if it's stolen and we find out, then you going to be in a lot more trouble. This your last chance to come clean."

I shook my head.

"Okay, I'm going to put you in the back of the car and see what happens."

He put me in the back of the squad car and I started thinking about it being something in the car that I don't know about. Then said *fuck it* and thought about my plan to get out this shit. It was at least five minutes before the police came back. One got in the driver's seat and the other one came to open the back door.

"Okay, you're clear on that so after we call the owner to make sure it ain't stolen and we run your name, you'll be able to get picked up by your parents, so just relax."

He got in the front, typed something in the computer, then turned and asked, "What's your name?"

I thought about giving the Lil Tone's name and have Mama T

come get me but I didn't know if I'd be able to talk to her, so I just gave them my real name. "John Thompson."

He typed my name in the computer. "Date of birth?"

"February 19, 1983."

It ain't take long for it to pull up that I was a runaway.

"So, John, where you been all these months?"

"A little of everywhere."

"It says that April should be with you. Where she at?"

"She went her own way and I went mine. We ain't talked since the first month."

"Well, we are going to go to the station and call your caseworker to come get you."

"What about the car?"

"It's going to be towed and the owner will have to get it."

I didn't have nothing else to say so I laid my head back and closed my eyes, but he still wanted to ask questions.

"So, why are you a runaway?"

"'Cause I didn't like the people they had me livin' with."

"What about your real parents?"

"I only had a mama and she got killed."

"That sucks."

For some reason we were still sitting there then after a few minutes, he asked, "So, how you been eating and stuff all this time, selling drugs?"

"Naw, I had a few jobs that paid in cash."

"Where have you been sleeping?"

"I got a few female friends. How long we gon' sit here?"

"The tow truck should be here soon."

I laid my head back again, hoping he'd leave me alone. I started thinking about getting shit in order once I get back home. Really, it was just April and Lil Tone because everybody else is in line so I had to get them right before the rest of the team started following in their footsteps.

I must have dozed off, because the next thing I knew they were waking me up at the Maywood police station.

I stood up and the one that was driving asked if I was tired.

"I guess so."

The other one asked if I was hungry.

"I'll be cool if I can buy some chips and juice."

"Okay, let's get you inside and processed. Then, we'll grab you something and you can get back to sleep."

We did it in that order and without even finishing my chips I was asleep.

"Mr. Thompson, somebody is here for you."

I was still half sleep and ain't hear shit he said. "What?"

"You're free to go."

"Oh."

I got up and grabbed my trash before following dude down the hall until we got to the front desk where Ms. Long was standing with my stuff.

"Long time no see, John. How have you been doing?"

"I'm good, ready to leave here."

"You're not going to run on me, are you?"

I didn't plan to run, but if she didn't drop me off at Corn crib then I'm going to get low on her. I grabbed my stuff off the counter and put it in my pockets. I put on my belt before I turned my cell phone back on.

"You won't be able to keep that at the place you going to."

"I guess I'll just have to give it to you then, but can I call somebody?"

"Okay, but only while I sign these papers, then, I get it back."

"Whatever."

I hit Corn up first so he can set up my plan.

"What's up?"

"What's good with it, homie?"

"Damn, where the fuck you at? You got everybody stressing."

"They lettin' me go but I only got a minute 'cause Amanda trippin."

"Oh shit, she came to pick you up. Do she know?"

"Naw, that's why I need you to call her and tell her to call my number 'cause I wanna get up with her, tonight. You got me?"

He started laughing. "You a fool, but I got you. Just wait like ten minutes. What about the blocks?"

"I'm about to call Blacky and have him handle everything so that should be good 'til I get back."

"Alright, let me go so you can do that and if you can, call April's crazy ass so she can stop calling my damn phone."

"I'll holla at you later."

I hung up and called Blacky.

"Yeah?"

"This Bishop."

"What's good, my nigga?"

"Shit, I'm just getting' out this jam, but I'm not gon' be back for probably a day, so I need you to handle that B.I. for me."

"What all you need me to do?"

"Pretty much the same shit you already do, but you'll need to keep tabs on whatever comes in and goes out, and I need you to stay at my crib 'til I get back so you can watch the block."

"My girl gon' start trippin', but I gotcha!"

"I 'preciate it, homie, and if you want we got an extra room so yo girl and kids can spend the night too."

"Alright but hurry the fuck up."

"I plan to and I got you for this."

"Don't trip."

We hung up and I got ready to call April but Ms. Long was finished.

"Okay, John, time to give it up."

She held out her hand but I wasn't about to give it to her, yet.

"One last call. I promise it'll only be a minute."

I pressed *Send* before she could answer.

"Hello."

"Let me talk to my girl."

"Bishop, you..."

I had to cut her off.

"Twin, I ain't got a lot of time."

I heard her yell and tell April I was on the phone and a few seconds later she was on the phone.

"Hey baby, where you at?"

"Don't act like shit ain't happen. I just wanted you to know I'm good and that I'ma get at you tomorrow."

"Don't be like that. I'm sorry, I didn't mean that shit."

"Okay, John, time's up." Ms. Long had her hand out again.

"Who was that?"

"That's my caseworker and I gotta go."

"I love you, baby."

"Okay."

I pressed *End*, but not before she yelled some more bullshit. I handed it to Ms. Long and she tried to turn it off.

"Can you keep it on so somebody can call back?"

"No, because you are not going to be planning to get away from me."

"You can answer it and just tell me what they say."

She thought about it before she said, "I'll put it on speaker for you, but you have to give me your word that you're not going to run on me."

"Okay, that's a deal."

CHAPTER FIFTEEN

She put the papers and phone in her purse and we walked out to the car.

"Where I'm goin' this time?"

"Someplace that'll make you wish you still were with the Davis family."

"I doubt it, but it don't matter. I'm ready to go."

It's hard to imagine anywhere worse than living with them people, but hopefully, I didn't have to find out.

"Do you know that you could've killed Tyrone with the way you beat him?"

"So?"

Before she could say anything else her phone rang.

She turned to me. "Hold on while I take this call."

She answered and I only heard her side, but I knew it was Corn.

"Hello... I'm doing good. Just picked up a client... in about two hours. Why?"

She turned red and started smiling from whatever he said. "Oh, really? That's good to hear. I will make that call now... okay, I'll talk to you later. Bye."

She hung up and placed her phone in the cup holder between us. "I have to make a quick call."

"But my friend should call soon."

"Don't worry. I'll be done fast."

"But what if she calls while you're on the phone?"

I smiled and thought about the way she sucked my dick, causing my dick to start rocking up.

I decided to stop playing games and got to it. I looked at her. "You don't even got to make that call. I know that you've been trying to get up with me. So, here's your chance."

"If you want to talk about why you ran away we can do that but let me make this call real quick."

"Amanda, you're callin' my phone. It was me that night with Corn."

We were at a red light and she caught on to what I said but she didn't believe me because she went in her purse and took my phone out. She called the number that Corn gave her and my phone rang. She hung up and pulled in the first gas station we came to.

Once she parked, she put her head on the steering wheel and start mumbling over and over, "I should've known."

I moved closer and put my arms around her but let go when she tensed up.

"Look, I know you wanna fuck, so let's go. If you want, I can drive."

"No, we are not going to do nothing but take you to the placement."

"You know that ain't happenin' so you might as well get what you want."

"It don't matter what I want. I can get in trouble and lose my job."

"Who gon' say somethin'?"

She ain't say nothing so I gave her my answer.

"I know I'm not."

I grabbed her hand and put it on my dick. Once she didn't move it, I knew she was going.

"Promise?"

"Yeah, I'll give you that promise."

"And you'll spend more nights with me?"

"I got a girl, but I'll get with you once a month."

"Every two weeks."

"Alright."

She looked at me and start rubbing my dick through my jeans, then said, "But you're only sixteen."

"Yeah, that's the same thing Ms. Davis said last year."

"She was having sex..."

"Let's not talk about that now," I said cutting her off.

"Okay, but I have to drop you off somewhere and make a report that you ran away from me."

"Why don't we get a hotel room for the night?"

"We can use my house."

"Maybe next time, but let's get a room around here so we don't waste time 'cause I got a lot of shit to do tomorrow. Plus, I'll pay, okay?"

"You're in charge. Where to?"

I told her to drive and we'll find one, which we did only a few blocks away. I gave her the money to check-in and went to the room after she went back to the station to make a report.

While she was gone, I called everybody to let them know that I'll be home for sure sometime the next day. Of course, April had a million questions, but I shut her up by telling her that it was her fault and she was lucky I'm coming back at all. After I knew I could chill, I jumped in the shower, then waited for Amanda to get back. I thought about leaving for a second, but the thought of treating her like the hoe she is and blowing her back out made me stay. It must have been about an hour that she left me waiting before it was a knock on the door.

I got up and opened the door to let her in. She smiled before she said, "I thought you might not be here when I got back."

"If yo ass would've took another minute I was gone, but I'm not here to talk."

I pushed her toward the bed and we got to it. I made her sit down facing me. I undid my pants and pulled my dick out. She looked at it like she wanted to swallow it whole, she tried to grab it but I stopped her and start slapping her in the face with it until she started moaning for it. I was only semi-hard but grew real quick when she started sucking it like she lived for it.

"Damn, shorty, you tryin' to make a nigga fall in love with yo head?"

"Umm, Uh."

"I hope you plan to swallow this shit."

"Mmmm."

She started sucking even better and I knew I wasn't going to last much longer. I grabbed the back of her neck and started fucking her mouth when I felt myself getting ready to nut, but instead of shooting down her throat I pulled out and coated her face with it.

Just like a nasty hoe she started wiping it off with her fingers and licked it off.

"You like that shit, don't you?"

"Yep. Can I get more?"

"Naw. I'm ready to hit that pussy, now, but you gotta go clean yourself up first."

"You want to shower with me?"

"I wish you'd stop talkin' so we can finish and I can go take care of my business."

She looked at me for a second like she wanted to say something stupid but thought better of it and went in the bathroom. I was starting to like her more because all her freak ass wanted to do is suck and fuck. So, I didn't have to deal with all that other shit like with April, plus I can have my way with her.

My thoughts were interrupted by her coming out the bathroom. This was my first time actually seeing her naked and I would've never thought those clothes she had on could hide a body like that. Thick, petite, her breast were perky. She had a lil shape to her.

"Damn, shorty. Yo body killin' shit."

She did a little spin, giving me a good view of how fat her ass was, making my dick do a little jump like it had a mind of its own.

"You like what you see, Daddy?"

I just looked down at my piece which made her laugh saying, "I guess you do."

"Come here."

She walked over to me and I put my hand by her pussy and opened her legs so I can dip my finger in. Seeing how wet she was, I pulled her on the bed with me and rolled on top of her. She grabbed my dick, guided it in, and threw her legs up on my shoulders.

I grabbed her hands and pinned them to the bed. I pulled

out and slammed back in, letting a few seconds pass before I did it again. Her pussy was so good I wanted to stay in it all night but time was precious and I had to get back on the block.

"Baby, let me get on top."

I don't know if she read my mind but I wanted to see that ass bounce on the dick. I rolled off her and laid on my back. She hopped on top, reverse cowgirl style, and started riding like it was a top competition.

"Oh, unh, oh yeah!"

She started screaming and moaning, then I felt her pussy start pulsing on my dick and every time she came up it was like a cup of water going down my piece.

I let her ride her wave for a little before pushing her off me so I could hit it from the back. She tried to get on all fours, but I pushed her head down so I can get all in her guts. She didn't even give me time to do my thing before she started throwing the pussy back at me. I grabbed her by the hip and started trying to blow her back out. I knew it wasn't going to last long and just as I was reaching that point, she reached back, grabbed my piece, and pulled me out.

"What the fuck?"

She rubbed it on her pussy a few times before moving it up to her asshole and pushed back, taking the whole dick in one stroke.

"Damn, shorty!"

I ain't never did this, but I started hitting it without missing a beat. Her moans had me ready to nut, but when she put her fingers in her pussy and matched my stroke. I couldn't take it no more and bust a fat ass nut. While I was getting my nut, she had another orgasm and fell forward with me still inside her.

When I got my mind right, I got up so I could clean up and go home but after taking another shower I walked out find shorty playing with her pussy.

"You ready for another round?"

Listening to my little head, how could I refuse?

CHAPTER SIXTEEN

"Shorty ain't ever want to let a nigga leave."

I just got done telling Corn what I did with Amanda while he drove me to the crib.

"Damn. She let you fuck her in the ass?"

"She ain't let me. Shorty put it in there and made me."

"That bitch a boss freak, real talk."

He ain't say shit for a minute so I start thinking about what I was going to say when I talked to April and Lil Tone.

"What you on now?"

"Man, I was just thinking that I had to get my shit straight at the crib and with my homie, 'cause they got me out here on the streets slippin'. I'm just lucky I left the banga at the crib."

"What you want to do about yo car?"

"Shit, if we get it back, I can't drive it 'cause them people know about it, so I'll just sell it and get a new one."

"You can buy the van if you want. I was gon' get rid of it anyways."

He had a clean ass cocaine white conversion van with everything on the inside.

"Hell yeah. I'll buy it. How much you want?"

"For you, I'll give it up for fifteen and you can keep the T.V. and Play Station but I'm keeping my sounds."

"Cool, let me call April and tell her to bring that money out or you can wait and I'll bring all yo shit out."

"How much you got?"

"It should be around twelve stacks for the work and shit, plus fifteen-hundred for the van."

Corn nodded. "So, how much I got to give you for the weed?"

"I already took that out."

"So, what we coppin' this time?"

"Shit, we all putting almost nine G's to get seventy-five."

"Alright, but I think we gon' run through that, so if you want, give me five stacks back. Put y'all piece in it and double that order."

"You think it's gonna move like that?"

"I got some shit lined up, but we gon' have to see."

We were pulling up in the alley and I was too happy to see that Blacky had shit moving like normal.

"That's what's up, then. I'm gonna holla at my homie and let him know the business, then tell you when to have the driver ready."

"Alright, I'll get that money when I drop the van off."

I gave him some dap and got out the car. I saw a few workers in the cut doing their thing and another one working security. It was Lil Tone's shift, but for some reason, I didn't expect to see his car and I was even more surprised when I walked on Washington and saw him posted on Loctus.

I walked up to him. "What's up, Joe?"

"Nothing, really. You good?"

"Yeah, but I need to holla at you in the crib so when you get somebody to take yo spot, come in."

"I'll be there in a minute."

I walked in the crib and stood in the doorway for a few seconds before one of the Twins said, "Lil Tone, that you?"

"Naw, it's me."

I walked in the living room and saw not only the Twins bagging up but Blacky and another female.

"What's good with y'all?"

"Hey, Bishop!" The twins said together.

"What's good with it, Bishop? This wifey I was always tellin' you about," Blacky said as he got up and gave me some dap.

I gave his girl a head nod, then asked, "Where the kids at?"

"In the room, sleep."

"What about April?" I asked, directed at the Twins, but Blacky answered.

"She went to lay down about an hour ago. She been awake since I got here."

"So, what's been up?"

"Everything been straight over here but the weed spots moving so fast two-block had to shut down twice and the other ones wasn't too far behind. Otherwise, shit went good."

"I was wondering why you was baggin' some weed up. So, how they lookin' out there now?"

"It's good now. We shouldn't run out again no time soon 'cause I had some of my people bag up a few pounds, plus we been going hard over here with the Twins."

"How much they want for helpin'?"

"Shit, I gave they ass a half of pound and they was good with that."

"So, I guess y'all don't need me then, huh?"

"Yeah, we do!" Everybody said at once.

"I don't think I'm ever going to want to be around that girl again if you ain't here," Lucky said. Chocolate skin. Petite. Short black hair gel'd to head. five-foot-six.

I was confused. "Who, April?"

Lucky nodded.

"Why you say that?"

"She was just trippin' hard."

What she said made me mad and made me want to go wake April up and snap on her. Lucky was Blacky's baby mama, a chocolate, petite, short broad who rocked her hair gel'd to her head. I liked her. She was cool, loyal and she genuinely supported Blacky, even when it had to do with what we had going on. April was out of line.

I turned toward the room, but Blacky grabbed me. "Hold up, let me holla at you outside."

I ain't want to but I followed him out.

"What's good?"

"Man, don't pay that shit no mind. April just let her emotions get the best of her but it was expected, given the situation."

"Man, she ain't about to get away with dissin' somebody that's trying to help me. She needs to learn to control her damn emotions."

Before he could say anything else, Lil Tone walked up.

"What's happenin'?"

"Shit, just give us a minute and we'll be inside."

When he closed the door, I turned back to Blacky. "You feel what I'm sayin' tho'?"

"Yeah, I feel you, just don't let that shit start no mo' problems with y'all."

"Alright, just 'cause you say so."

I was about to go back in but stopped. "Man, I appreciate you comin' through for me. When I get this money count taken care of I'm gonna hit you."

"It ain't shit, homie."

We went back in and I headed to my room to get April up but ran into Lucky coming out the extra room.

"Is it okay if we spend the night because I don't want to get these kids up, then have to put them back to sleep?"

"You ain't even got to ask no question like that. Make yo'self at home."

"Thank you, Bishop."

"It ain't shit," I said and then walked in my room.

I sat there and watched April sleep for a few seconds and thought about letting her sleep, but I had to get this bullshit out the way.

"Ay shorty, get up."

She rolled over and when she saw me, she said, "Baby, I'm sorry. Don't be mad at me."

"Shorty, I ain't mad but me, you and Lil Tone about to sit down and have a talk, so go get yo shit together so we can get this out the way."

She got up out the bed and came to kiss me before she left out.

I went to check on the stash to see if they took care of the money like I told them to.

When April walked back in, I left to get Lil Tone. He was in the front room smoking a cigarette, which had apparently become a bad habit for him now.

"Let me holla at cha' now, but put that square out before you come in the back."

If it wasn't for the Twins, it wouldn't be no smoking in my crib but now it's only allowed upfront.

Lil Tone was right behind me as I walked in the room so I told him, "Close the door behind you."

April was sitting on the bed. I went and sat down on the edge of the dresser.

Lil Tone closed the door and posted up beside it. "What's good with it, bruh?"

"Man, I'm tryin' to figure out why the two people I care about the most are the ones that are bringing me the most problems."

"What you mean by that, baby?"

"Exactly what I said, shit! He's out there tryin' to chase pussy while he suppose to be watchin' over the block, and you get to trippin' on some petty shit, then start actin' like a kid. That shit stressing me the fuck out. Y'all suppose to be the ones that got my back, but y'all cause me to slip and almost get locked up in some crazy hospital and lose everything I worked hard to build."

Lil Tone rubbed his temples and threw his arms up in exasperation. "I mean, I said my bad, shit. What else you want me to do...get on my knees and beg you to forgive me?"

I damn near went off and hit him in his mouth for saying that shit but thought better of it because I was trying to solve the problem, not make a new one.

"Man, I'm gon' act like you ain't even say that shit. I don't have no family to turn to. Y'all still got y'all people that's gon' be there, but if I fuck this up, it's back to a foster home or a place like they was gonna send me today and I'm not goin' like that."

April squinted her eyes and sucked her teeth. "How you

going to act like I'm going to leave you out here by yourself if something go wrong. If I have to depend on my mommy and daddy, then you coming with me."

"And you know my ol' G ain't gonna deny you shit, so you can stop trippin'."

"That's the point. If y'all the ones to bring me down, then why the fuck would I want to stay with y'all? When the fuck have y'all seen me just sit back and depend on somebody? I'm out to get my own and I don't need my own people holding me back."

"Alright man, what you tryin' to say?" Lil Tone folded his arms across his chest and squinched his lips to the side.

"If y'all fuckin' up, then the workers gon' start fuckin' up, too. Lil Tone, I need you to act like you did when we started with a few pounds of weed, and April, I don't need you acting like a little ass girl when shit don't go yo way. It's gon' be times that I need space, don't take the shit personal."

We sat in silence for a moment, all in our own thoughts until April said, "Baby, I got your back and no matter what, you can come to a peaceful home. My people taught me the game and I know how to play my part."

"Yeah, bruh, I got you. Don't even trip, I'm back on business. All that other shit out the window."

"That's what's up, but y'all gotta make me a believer. Since we got that out the way, I been up too long so I'm about to get some sleep."

"Alright, I'll holla at you later, homie."

"Yup, but on yo way out tell Blacky I need to holla at him."

Lil Tone walked out April said, "You okay now, baby?"

"Yeah, when I get some sleep."

I knew I needed some sleep but the main reason I wanted to go was so she didn't try to have make up sex. I'm all fucked out.

"How you get away from your caseworker? Ran from her?"

More like ran through her. "Somethin' like that."

Blacky walked in, "What's good?"

I grabbed the 9mm off the dresser. "Man, I need you to hold the banga down 'cause I'm 'bout to lay it down."

"Alright, we probably bag up for a few mo' hours. Then I'll drop the Twins off unless they stayin' the night."

"Man, that's a good look but you'll have to ask 'em what they doin'. I got you and yo girl in the morning, y'all helped a nigga too much."

I really ain't want to admit it but when it came down to it, I trust Blacky over Lil Tone now.

"I told you it ain't shit. I'll be posted by the time you get up, so I'll holla then."

"Alright, homie."

I had already taken a shower, so after closing the door I took off my clothes and got in bed. April did the same and kissed me.

"I truly love you, baby."

That was the last thing I heard before I passed out.

CHAPTER SEVENTEEN

"What's happening, hustler?"

I was walking up to Hectic's crib when, like always, he was at the door before I knocked.

"Man, it's happenin' but it's a lot that comes with it."

"Yeah, I heard about you getting' popped."

"That ain't even part of it. Shit, that might've been a good thing compared to the rest of the bullshit I'm goin' through."

"Well, let's sit down and rap about it."

We went and sat down in our normal seats but Hectic jumped back up.

"You want a beer?"

"Naw, I'm good."

I almost wanted to say 'yeah,' but I didn't want to depend on that when I start having problems.

Hectic came back, opened a bottle, then he said, "So, what's up?"

I wasted no time telling him just about everything. When I

was done, he ain't say nothing... just sat there and drank on his third beer for a few minutes.

Finishing the beer, he sat it on the table. "But you failing to say one of the most important things that's eating you up."

"What cha' mean?"

"It's plain and simple that you don't trust Lil Tone no more."

When I ain't say shit he asked, "Right?"

"Yeah, I guess but..."

"It ain't no buts, he fucking up. Do you still trust yo girl?"

"Yeah, I trust her."

"And this other guy, Blacky?"

"That's the thing. I trust him more than I do Lil Tone."

"Look, you ain't doing nothing wrong, homie. Some guys ain't always going to be able to perform at the plate, so you have to put a pinch hitter in and just have him do what he can. Don't let one player make you lose the game, no matter how much you like him."

I thought about what he said before asking, "So I should take him off the block?"

"That really depends."

"On what?"

"If that's what you want to do."

"I don't know."

"Then when you find that out, I can give you some options to work with but 'til then you just have to go with the flow."

"I think I owe it to him to give him a lil' time to prove he ain't playin' no mo', you feel me?"

"That's on you, but you don't owe nobody nothing, only yourself. The main thing you owe yourself is to keep it real."

It really wasn't nothing else for me to say so I waited for him to keep going.

"Okay, with that out of the way, what's with the business? You want one fifty, right?"

"Yeah."

"I see y'all doing it real big out there."

"On some real shit, I ain't even think we were gon' get it movin' this quick, but everybody want yo shit."

"I never doubted you. I saw the potential the first time you came over, but I ain't even see you gettin' this big. You gettin' paid."

"We hope to keep goin' like this but we're tryin' something out and hope it works out."

"How long 'til yo people get here?"

I look at my watch before I answered, "In about fifteen minutes."

"I'm sure the money counts on point but let me go count it before they get here so we can load up and get them back moving."

I gave him the bag with the money and he went to the back room. It was about ten minutes before he came back out and nodded his head at me.

"Alright, let me go out and see how far out they are," I said as I got up and went to the door.

"I'm about to pull around back, so just wait back there."

We never switched here no more because he ain't want to keep that much weed at his crib but I knew it had to do with the drivers and not wanting them to know where he lived or kept his stash because we followed him to a different spot every time.

I opened the door but Hectic stopped me. "What's up?"

"They pulling through the alley, come with me out front."

We went out the front door and I finally saw the T.V. screens showing the whole block, letting me know how he knew I was there before I got to the door. We got in the car and drove to the alley where I jumped out and went up to the first car, which was the one that always came so I knew she was good.

I don't know where Corn got them from but he had a team of white females as the drivers and this time it was five cars.

When she let the window down, I said, "They all know what's up, right?"

"I told them all that they need to know."

"That's what's up. So, you ready to ride?"

"Yeah."

I went and got in the van I bought from Corn and pulled up behind Hectic. We rode about fifteen minutes but only ended up about three blocks from his crib. He slowed to a stop in front of the crib, then turned on the left turn signal, letting me know to pull to the back of that house.

The females never got out the car. They pulled up, popped the trunk and Hectic's people loaded them up while I watched and counted how many went in each car. Re-up complete, I led them back to the highway. It was in Corn's hands from there. I called him to let him know everything was good on my end.

I drove back to the crib and was greeted by April when I entered.

She gave me a hug and kiss. "Hey, baby. How'd everything go?"

"Shit, it went as planned. What's up here?"

"Nothing, but I do need to talk to you in private."

I went in the living room to say what's up to the twins before I followed April to the room.

"What's good?"

"I just wanted to let you know that I hired Lucky to help me out some."

"What? You can't handle the lil work that I ask you to do or you just getting' lazy?"

I started to get mad but didn't because when it's all said and done, I was going to be getting mine.

"It ain't even like that. She's been over here the last few days without really doing nothing so I asked her to help me so now during the day while she do my rounds I can help you out and you can worry about the bigger stuff."

I thought about it for a second and saw that it was a good idea.

"Come here."

She walked over and I pulled her in my arms and started kissing her but stopped long enough to say, "Thanks for having my back, shorty."

I walked her over to the bed and laid her down.

I started taking my clothes off when she said, "Baby, the Twins out there."

"So, they know we fuck and if you so worried, then don't make so much noise with all that screaming."

I laughed as I laid next to her and started taking her clothes off too.

"Funny boy."

I started kissing her and playing with her pussy until I felt her wet and ready before I climbed on top of her.

Before I entered her, she said, "Beat this pussy up, baby."

From the moment I put the dick in her, she was moaning like crazy and throwing her hips back at me with every stroke which caused both of us to get off in minutes. After I held her for a few more minutes I got up, put my shit back on, then went in the bathroom and cleaned myself up. Just when I was finished April walked in, covering herself with her clothes.

"Baby, your phone ringing."

"Who is it?"

"I didn't answer it."

"Why not?"

"Because that's your phone and you ain't tell me to answer it."

I heard it ringing still so I ran to get it.

"What's good?"

"Whats up, homie. You good, right now?"

It was Corn but I realized that it could've been Amanda and was happy that April ain't make a habit of answering my phone.

"Yea, what's up? I was just in the other room."

"Well, I just wanted to let you know that everything touched down."

"That's what's up. So, what we on now?"

"I got a few people that want some for nine hundred each but they comin' for a sawbuck or better. I still got some niggas to holla at so hopefully we'll finish this quick"

"That's what's up then. Just tell me what you want me to do."

"Bet." He paused before asking, "You remember ol' boy we went to holla at that day up north?"

"The one with the bitch, right?"

"Yeah, him."

"What about him?"

"That nigga snapped last night and killed that bitch, then blew his own shit off."

"Damn! That's fucked up, he was with that same bitch?"

"Dude was a sucka, lil homie. He ain't even kick her out."

"Well, betta him than me."

"Same shit I said."

April came in the room and was waiting for me and as on cue, Corn said, "Man, I'll hit you up later. I got another call."

"Alright. I'll get at you then."

I hung up and turned to April and asked, "What you on now?"

"Nothing really. Why?"

"Shit, since you wanna help, why don't you start checkin' the books and make sure everything is right, you can start doing that tomorrow."

"Okay. I'll just bag up with the twins then."

"I'm about to chill on the block for a lil bit."

I grabbed the black 9mm out of the dresser and put it in the front of my pants, then walked out towards the front door. When we got by the living room the twins said at the same time, "Must've been nice," and started laughing.

April hit me on the chest. "I told you."

I walked out the crib laughing, knowing they was about to grill her.

CHAPTER EIGHTEEN

"Baby, wake up." April was shaking me, trying to get me up but I just rolled over.

"Give me about an hour, shorty. I'm tired as hell."

"Baby, something ain't right. You need to go check on the block."

That caught my attention and I sat up. "What's wrong?"

"I don't know. It's just this funny feeling I got."

"Man, carry yo silly ass back to bed with that shit." I looked at the clock to see that it was 4:07 in the morning and laid back down.

"If you ain't going to check, then I will." She got up and went to put some pants on, but I stopped her.

"I swear I ain't got time for this shit April, but if it makes you feel better, I'll check. Go get my boots and coat out the closet."

I really didn't want to get up but I knew April was thick-headed and would've went out there.

I got up and put some jeans on, then got the 9mm and made sure it was ready to go. April brought my boots and coat once I had everything on. I told April to stay home until I got back.

She nodded and I left the room. I didn't even put the banger on my waist; I kept it in hand, just in case.

As soon as I opened the front door, I started getting the feeling that something was not right and after checking the whole block, I realized wasn't nobody out there.

"Bitch ass nigga."

It's been about a good five months since the last incident with Lil Tone and I thought he was down now, but I should've known it was just a matter of time and he'd go back to his old tricks.

I was walking back towards the crib when I ran across a group of cluckas, "Ay nephew, how long before y'all back up? This ain't a twenty foe no mo'?"

"Yeah, it's still the same. Something just happened tonight, but if y'all give me a few minutes I gotcha."

I went back in the crib and yelled to April, "Ay baby, can you bring my phone out here for me?"

I went to the spot and grabbed a bundle out, then dumped the packs on the table.

"Baby, what's wrong?" She asked as she handed me the phone.

I had Lil Tone on speed dial so I only had to press one button to call him.

As I heard the first ring I answered April, "Ain't nobody on the block. This nigga back playin' them bitch ass games."

After about the sixth ring it went to his voice mail, so I hung up.

"So, what we about to do?"

"Shit, it's some clucks out there waitin' now so I'm about to post up 'til Blacky get here."

"Let me get dressed and I'll be out there in a minute."

I really didn't like the idea of her being out there but I did need the extra eyes so I agreed.

I grabbed three packs off the table and went outside again. The group of cluckas was still in the alley where I left them, I gave them an extra bag for waiting. I went to the front so I could catch as much of the block as I could. We were out there working the block for about forty minutes and for every customer I served, I asked when was the last time they saw Lil Tone but none of them knew shit.

A female clucka came and asked was he alright, I asked her why she asked that.

"I was on my way over there around like three something but I was about a block away and I saw the jump out boys had some-body stretched out so I turned around."

"Did you see if it was him?"

"Naw, because they had whoever it was face down."

"Alright, how many you lookin' for TT?"

She handed me her money. "Give me five."

I went in my pocket and gave her ten and her eyes got big like she already took a hit. "Thank you, nephew."

No sooner did she walk off did I see this nigga walking up the block. I wait for him to get closer before I asked, "Where the fuck you been?"

"Man, I tried calling you but you ain't pick up."

I looked at my phone, knowing it wasn't no missed calls on it when April gave it to me.

"So, where the fuck you been at?"

"Shit, I was the only one on the block so I said fuck it and went to this bitch crib I met the other night."

I couldn't even control myself. I hit him in his face three times, making him stagger back a little. I was about to keep going at him but April jumped in front of me.

"So, you wanna fight me now, Bishop?"

"I told you about that bullshit and I'm not goin' to no mo'."

"Yeah, I guess I did deserve that but I tried callin' you and..."

"Nigga, stop lyin'! It wasn't no missed calls on my phone! Why you ain't just use yo key and come wake me up or at least put my money on the table?"

When he just stood there looking at me, I said, "Right 'cause you back on that dumb shit. You lucky I don't just kick you off the block but you ain't runnin' it no mo' so now you got all the freedom to come and go as you please but you sellin' packs."

"That's what it is now?"

The nigga looked like he was ready to cry but I didn't give a fuck.

"You fuckin' up my money, so hell yeah. Matter of fact, where my shit at now?"

He got some money and work out then handed it to April.

"That count betta be on point, too. Get out my face and don't come back around for a few days."

He started walking away but April stopped him, "Lil Tone, you don't know about the police being over here?"

"Naw, that must of happened after I left, it ain't have nothing to do with us."

When nobody said nothing else, he walked off and got in his car, which I just noticed since I been out here.

When he peeled off, April walked over to the corner with me.

"Baby, you okay?"

"It's fucked up but yeah, I'm good. Just might have to put in mo' work now."

"Don't trip on that. We can hold this down."

And that's what we did until Blacky and some workers got there, and every day for the next three weeks they did.

CHAPTER NINETEEN

"Who this is?"

Somebody been blowing my phone up for the last ten minutes from an unknown number. I got tired of letting it ring and picked it up.

"Lil homie, I need to holla at cha'."

It was Corn but it sounded like he was trying to change his voice.

"What's good with it?"

"Ain't no talkin on the phone right now, come to the Central Train Station."

"Alright, give me like five minutes."

I hung up and called April in the room.

When she got here, I said, "I'm about to holla at Corn but I don't' know when I'll be back."

"Okay, just hit me up if you need me."

"Alright, I'll be back when I can." I kissed her and left.

Outside, the sky was a charcoal grey, and the sun's absence

was being felt. I blew in my hands and rubbed them together as I walked towards the train station. I tried thinking about what Corn wanted but couldn't think of nothing, except something wasn't right. It was cold outside, and once I got to the station and paid for a pass, I walked up the stairs. Corn was waiting there for me but didn't say shit when I walked up to him, just gave me some dap.

We stood there waiting until the first train came. Then we got on.

As soon as we pulled off, I asked, "What's good?"

"Man, it's getting hot, lil homie."

Oblivious to what he was saying I said, "Yeah, I know. This summer we gon' take this bitch over."

Corn started laughing before he said, "Damn, I needed that but I'm talking about these people getting' hot."

"Damn!"

"I don't know if they on to you but they on my heels. Have you been seeing anybody watchin' the block?"

"Naw, but to keep it real I ain't been watchin' like that."

"They probably don't want you anyway but you gotta be on yo shit from now on, just in case."

I ain't know what to say so I asked the obvious question, "What now?"

"Man, it's only a matter of time before they come holla at me, so I'm trying to stash as much money as I can but when it's re-up time, I'm not doin' shit."

"What about the weed?"

He thought about it for a second before he said, "I think you good so we'll keep that movin'. I'm shuttin' my spot down this week and puttin' everything over there with you 'til it runs out. Then, we ain't goin' to keep that open twenty-four no more."

"How we gon' do it, then?"

"When shit start pickin' up in the morning?"

"Like at four-five o'clock."

"And when it slow down?"

"Shit, it's hard to say. Maybe around eight."

"Then the block gon' open at four and close at eight, for the ones that spend good money. They can call you and you meet them."

"Alright, I'll change that up in about two days."

I thought about what's going to happen when or if he gets locked up and asked him, "What you need me to do if they pick you up?"

"I'm taking some money to my lawyers and for the most part, they goin' to keep me good. Then my ol' G will handle the rest. I need you to keep a clear head so when I need you, you can handle street shit for me."

"Alright, I got you. Just let me know."

We were pulling up to a station when Corn stood up. "I got to go, but keep yo eyes open."

I got off at the next stop and switched trains to go back home. I was hungry so I stopped at Taco Queen across the street from the train station and ordered everybody burritos. Walking back to the crib, I thought about what Corn said and in so many words he told me at the end that it ain't *if* they picked him up—it's *when* they pick him up.

I get on the block and ran into Blacky.

"What's good, my nigga?"

"Shit, out here freezin' my ass off."

"You ain't gotta be out here."

"Naw, I'm good, but I hope you got something for a nigga to eat in that bag."

"I got everybody the same thing, get a pop or juice out the crib."

"Naw this good, good lookin'."

"Let me go in before I freeze with yo ass. When you get a chance, come holla at me."

"Alright, give me about an hour, if it can wait that long?"

"That's cool."

I go in the crib and found the twins and Lucky in the front room bagging up.

"What's up, y'all?"

"Hey, Bishop." One twin said followed by the other. "What you got in that bag?"

"Damn twins, that's how you greet a nigga?"

"I'm sayin, you come in with a bag smelling all good and shit, I'm hungry."

"Where April at?"

"She in the back."

I took our food out and gave them the rest of it.

"Y'all lucky I like y'all a lil bit, 'cause I was gonna' eat all that."

The twin's high asses just started laughing but Lucky shook her head and smiled. I went in the kitchen and grabbed a juice and a bottle of flavored water for April.

I walked in the room to find April counting money and putting it in the book.

"How it's looking?"

She looked up and smiled. "Hey, baby, we still killin' it."

"That's what's up."

"How Corn doing?"

"We'll talk about it but let's eat first."

I handed her her food and she said, "Boy, you know I can't

eat a whole one of these. Why you ain't just grab me a few tacos?"

"Stop complainin' and eat what you can and I'll eat the rest later. They better cold anyway."

We sat there and ate and when she start wrapping the rest of her food up I told her, "The police on Corn back."

She stopped and looked at me, "Stop playin'?"

"You know I ain't about to play with no shit like that. That's what he told me."

"That crazy. Did he say if it's state or Feds?"

"I ain't even think to ask that, so I don't know."

"So, what we gon' do?"

"Shit really, it's gon' be a few changes startin' with you not touchin' nothin' outside the crib. Then this block closin' after all the work is gon' but 'til then we changin' the hours from foe to eight and I'm gonna be makin' some moves off the phone."

"So, after that, it's over?"

"Naw, we still got the weed blocks and a lot of money put up."

It was a knock on the door.

"What up?"

"It's me. You ready to holla at me?"

"Yeah, come in."

Blacky walked in and April asked, "You want me to leave?"

"Naw shorty, you good.

I turn to Blacky, "Man, you think you can change up yo hours some?"

"Whatcha talkin' about?"

I told him everything that was going on.

"So, you want me to work from four to eight?"

"Yeah, pretty much."

"I guess I can do it but I got to pick up the kids and Lucky 'cause they ain't waking up at three in the morning."

"What you gon' do after this shit over?"

"Probably get a job and chill with the family."

"Alright, but if you ever need something, just holla at me."

He nodded his head and walked out, leaving me in thought of what I'd do next. All I really knew was the streets, and knew that I'd have to figure something out.

CHAPTER TWENTY

oom. Boom. Boom. Boom.
   I was just getting up when I heard four shots right outside the crib. I hurried and grabbed my gun, then put some sweatpants and shoes on.

"Baby, was that somebody shooting?"

I grabbed the .22 revolver that I bought from this clucka and handed it to April.

"If somebody come through this door and they don't announce who they is, pull the trigga, alright?"

"Okay."

I expected her to be scared but when she took the gun, she looked like she was ready for whatever. I ran to the front door, knowing she was going to be okay.

I opened the door but wasn't nobody there, so I ran out looking for Blacky, knowing he got here on time today. He wasn't in the alley but as I ran past the third slot of row houses, I saw him lying on the ground covered in blood. I ran up to him and saw that he was still breathing so I ran back to the front door.

"April, call the ambulance. Blacky got shot!"

I ran back to Blacky. "Man, don't die on me homie, yo family need you."

I start searching him so he wouldn't have shit on him when they picked him up. I got his phone and banga. He had no money or work.

"Lucky." I didn't get what he was saying at first so I moved my ear closer to him. "Call Lucky."

I took his phone and went through the numbers until I found Lucky's. She picked up on the third ring and I could tell she was still sleep.

"Lucky, I need you to be cool, alright?"

"That you, Bishop? Where Blacky?"

"Look, he just got shot and..."

"Tell me he's alright, Bishop! Please! I can't lose him!"

"Lucky, chill out. I need you to listen."

When she was calm enough to listen I said, "He still alive but he fucked up. He can't talk but I'm gon' put the phone on speaker and put it by him. I need you to keep talking to him 'til the ambulance get here and when they do, tell them not to take him to Loretta, that he need to go to Mount Sinai. You got that?"

It took her a second to answer so I called her name.

"Yeah, I got it."

"Alright. I got to go. They almost here and we on our way to get you right now." I put the phone on speaker, then said, "Stay strong. I need you to pull through so we can get the bitch nigga that did this. Now, here's Lucky."

I put the phone by him and ran back to the crib.

"April, everything good but get dressed. We got to go get Lucky and we takin' yo car since it's parked on Pine."

I walked in the room to find her already dressed but looking for something on the dresser.

"I can't find my keys."

"Mine right by the door. Just go get the car started. I'll be ready in a second."

I had some blood on the shit I was wearing so I changed, then grabbed a few G's to put in my pocket. I could hear sirens so I knew I had to get out of there quick before I got caught up and had to give the police my name. I locked the door and just as I hit the alley an ambulance and fire truck was pulling up. When they got out they ain't know where to go.

"He in the third slot!" I yelled.

They looked my way for a quick second, then went where I told them. I ran to where the car was and saw April in the passenger seat so I got behind the wheel.

"Sorry, baby. I'm too nervous to drive."

I didn't even respond... just pulled off and got out of there. When I looked in the rearview mirror, I saw two police cars fly past.

"Fuck! Baby, that nigga better not die on me."

"He going to make it, baby. Don't even trip."

"I didn't get why they had to shoot him, though. They got the money and work."

As I thought about it, he would've woke me up if nobody was out there to look out for him so who was it and why wasn't he still out there?

"Damn, I gotta call Corn." I got my phone and hit Corn's number.

"Man, what the fuck happened over there?"

"Somebody robbed and shot Blacky."

"That's fuckin' crazy, Joe. Is he good?"

"To be real, he fucked up bad. I hope he can pull through."

"I was just getting ready to call you."

"Why, what up?"

"My lawyer holla'd at them people and I'm turnin' myself in today."

"What the fuck is it about today and can it be worse? Shit, my day ain't even suppose to had started yet."

"Yeah, it's fucked up and if I could I'll stay out one mo' day. I would but if I don't go in they'll think I'm runnin' plus they got people watchin'. Y'all stay up, though, and don't forget the little people when y'all get big. Tell my lil sister I said I'll talk to her later."

I know he was trying to lighten shit up but when you close to losing one of your homies by death and the other one to the system, it ain't much that can make a nigga feel better.

"Man, let me know when it's good for me to holla at you."

"I'm gon' have my ol' G get at you soon."

"Alright, Big Homie, be easy. Talk to April before you go."

As I drove my mind flashed to the other bad day I had in my life. I started praying that it ain't end like that one. Hopefully, it's a God to answer.

I pulled up to Blacky's crib and saw April was crying.

I wiped the tears off her face and kissed her. "Don't even trip shorty. This shit gon' be behind us and we gon' be back movin'. Stay here and I'll go help Lucky with the kids, alright?" She nodded and I got out the car.

I knocked on the door and it was like Lucky was waiting right there. She flung the door open midway through my knock with her coat in hand. The first thing I heard was the kids crying.

"It's like they know something is wrong with their daddy," she said.

"Is they ready to go?"

"They won't let me dress them." She looked like she was ready to break down any second and that ain't something I need right now.

"Don't even worry about it. Just go wait in the car."

She just looked at me without moving like she expected me to say something else so I said the only thing that came to mind. "He gon' be alright."

That seemed to be what she wanted to hear. She put on her coat and went to the car. I followed the sounds to the kid's room because I had never been inside the house before. They were sitting on the floor and clothes, pampers and other kid stuff was all over the place. Deciding whose clothes were whose, I was able to clean them up and dress them. I put together a bag with some extra shit and something for them to snack on until we could feed them.

Putting everything in the car I asked Lucky, "Where they say they took him?"

"They say they'll take him to the one you told me but they might transfer him to UIC or Northwestern."

"Alright."

I wanted to hurry up and get there just in case they did move him but mainly so we can leave before the police get to asking questions. We were a couple minutes away and I was getting ready to update Lucky but April got to it first.

"Lucky, you know we only can stay for a few minutes before we got to go, right?"

I looked in the rearview mirror and saw that she was confused. I ain't want no funny shit running through her mind so I explained. "We can't stay 'cause the police gon' ask our names and you know that we on the run so we can't risk that, but we'll keep the kids for you."

"What if they move him? I need somebody to be with me."

I knew she wasn't going to be able to handle this by herself and I thought of who I can get to come and be with her. The only people that I could think of were the twins.

"I can try callin' the twins and have them come down here."

"That'll be cool. I just can't be by myself."

We were pulling up in front of the emergency room entrance so I told them, "Y'all go in while I call the twins and park. Leave the kids. I'll bring them with me."

As soon as I stopped, they jumped out and ran in the hospital. I started looking for a parking spot and called the twins who said they were on the way to the house and going to be waiting.

I parked, went inside with the kids, and was informed that Blacky was in surgery. I asked Lucky did she want to ride back to the crib with us so she ain't have to be alone but she said she wanted to stay in case anything happened. Letting her know to call as soon as anything changed, we left and drove to the crib in silence. The twins were waiting when we got there.

April took the kids inside and when I walked in, she asked, "What we doing today?"

"I got too much on my mind to do anything so everything shut down unless you feel like doin' it."

"These kids going to take my time up and I don't know how to drive that big ass van, plus, I'm too nervous."

"Alright, I'm gonna call Baby D and have her let everybody

know that we ain't doing shit for three days but we gonna holla at 'em tomorrow."

There was a knock on the door and I looked at April who shrugged her shoulders. I wasn't expecting nobody and after what happened this morning, I knew I had to be on point so I went to get my gun.

I came out the room and stood on the side of the door. "Who is it?"

"Man, it's me, Lil Tone."

I opened the door. "Where the fuck yo key at?"

He saw the banga and his eyes got big. "What's going on?"

"It's been a fucked up day. Somebody robbed Blacky, then shot him up."

"Damn, somebody killed Blacky. That's crazy, man."

"Naw, he ain't dead. Some bitch nigga just hit him a few times and when I find out who did it, I'm that nigga."

"I'm sayin', can I work the block?"

I thought about it. "Naw, it's gon' be hot and I don't want nothing else goin' down, so shit shut down for a few days."

"Yeah, I feel you."

He looked around and when he saw April he nodded his head towards her, then said, "I guess I get at you later. My moms should be at the crib now so I can get in my car."

"Alright, be cool."

"Yup, get at me if you need me."

CHAPTER TWENTY-ONE

As he left and I thought about what he said, he was the only nigga I had left but I really don't trust or believe he'll have my back. My thoughts were interrupted by my phone ringing.

"Yeah?"

"Bishop, he just got out of surgery, but they won't let me see him."

"Is he good?"

"He still living; that's all I want."

"Is the twins there?"

"Yeah."

"Put one of 'em on the phone."

After a few seconds, one of them gets on, "What's up, Bishop?"

"Ay, was you there when the doctor told Lucky what's up?"

"Yeah, he said that Blacky got shot three times. Once in the stomach, chest and head. The one to the head didn't go in tho' but the other two made him lose a lot of blood before he got here and that's what fucked him up."

"So, he gon' live, right?"

"He really ain't say. Just that he in a coma but if he can make it these next few days he got a good chance."

"Alright, after they let her see him, bring her to the crib and if anything happens, call me."

"I got cha'." We hung up and I told April what they said.

"I guess that's better than nothing, but I want to hear that he's woke and talking."

She made the kids something to eat and was cleaning up while their food cooled down.

"Homie, gon' be good." I said. "He made it this far."

"I'm about to feed these babies but when I'm finished you want me to cook you something?"

"I can't even think about food right now, shorty."

I went and sat on the couch in the living room with the kids and played with them until April brought the food. Then I helped feed them.

Finished, I got up and told April I was about to go handle some business but to holla at me if she needed a break or something.

"Okay, baby, I'll be here.

A Week Later

"Baby, we don't have too much work left."

"Yeah, I know. I was just thinkin' about that."

"Well, whatever you do, you got to make it happen soon because we going to run out in a few days."

Me and April were lying in bed after she gave me some head. I thought about what I can do to keep the block open and only one thing came to mind.

"I'm goin' to holla at Hectic in two days. I'm gonna see if he can hook me up with a good deal on some cocaine."

"Me and Lucky taking the kids and going to see Blacky. You coming?"

Ever since that incident took place, we let Lucky and the kids move in the other room and every day we take them to see Blacky. For the first few days, I went but when I opened the block back up, I've been posted up from open to close.

"Yeah, I'll go if y'all wait 'til around three."

"I'll let Lucky know."

"They ain't sayin' nothin' new?"

"No, not really. Just that it's up to him now."

I rolled over, got out of bed and got my fit ready for the day.

As I was about to go to the bathroom April said, "Unless you need me, I'm staying in bed a little longer."

"It ain't nothin' for you to do 'til it's time to make the drops on the weed block."

"I'll be up for that."

I went and handled my business in the bathroom, then got a few bundles out to hit the block but before I went out, I looked in on April. I thought she was sleep but when I was leaving out, she said, "Baby, don't forget your gun."

I damn near slipped and was about to leave without my banga. I walked to the dresser and got it. Turning the safety off, I put it on my waist.

"Good lookin', Shorty." I left out.

The sky was getting a little light in it and a few niggas was out waiting to get down. I busted down the first bundle and gave all of them two packs. April's car was parked in the alley so I sat on the hood and watched everything that happened. I only got up from that spot twice and that was to put some money up and grab another bundle. At about eight everything was moving like always.

I saw the first car coming down the alley. Then about six more hit the block from every way. I thought it was the police and didn't see no point in fighting or trying to run but when I saw a bunch of niggas that looked like they were from the hood I jumped off the car and pulled my banga out, then tried to hit the gangway but they already had somebody blocking them.

I didn't even think about trying to shoot my way out because everybody that jumped out the cars had to hold their guns with two hands.

One of the niggas that got out walked over to me and tried to take my 9mm but when I pulled it out his reach he said, "Lil homie, don't turn this into sumin' that it ain't."

I wasn't ready to die over a little money so I gave him the banga.

He said something in his phone, then turned back to me. "Somebody wanna holla at cha."

He nodded his head and all the other nigga pointed their guns down and moved off to the side. It was a few seconds before I saw a Cadillac riding down the alley.

It came to a stop and the dude that took my banga asked if I was Bishop.

I nodded and he said, "Go get in the back seat."

I ain't see no choice. I opened the door and saw wasn't nobody in the back seat. I got in.

It was two niggas in the front but only the passenger turned around and asked, "You know who I am?"

He was brown-skinned with beady eyes, deep 360 waves and a full but neatly trimmed facial hair. I could tell he had some size on him, too. Not fat, but like he lifted weights.

"Naw, I don't know who you is and I don't know why you fuckin' with me either."

He did a little laugh. "They call me, Cash."

"I heard of you but what's up?"

"This what it is lil nigga, I run this area... the whole L-Town and whatever happens over here, I want a piece of it."

"You got me fucked up, homie! Why you ain't come with this shit when my big homie was out?"

"Who, Corn?" When I ain't answer his question he said, "He must ain't get the time to tell you about payin' yo dues, but you betta believe that you ain't been out here all this time for free. Look, you still got the rest of the month but after you payin' five stacks for this block and a stack for each of them weed spots."

"Man, I'm not about to give you no twelve G's for nothing. I ain't goin' out like that."

"Don't worry about it. Just make sure all the blocks shut down by the first and if they're not I'll have some of my little niggas come do it for you. We done."

I got out the car and they drove off. The rest of the niggas except the one that had my banga jumped back in the cars and drove off.

I walked over to him. "Can I get my shit back now?"

He took the clip out, then popped the one out the chamber and only gave the gun back. He went and got in his car and when he turned out the alley, he tossed the rest of it out in the dirt.

I was mad as hell because this nigga came over here and just tried to treat me like a bitch nigga and I couldn't even do shit. I went to pick up my clip and the bullet I had in the chamber. I put it back in the banga, then put it on my waist again.

The pack workers walked up to me and asked, "You good, homie?"

"Yeah, y'all straight?"

"Man, if them niggas wasn't so deep, I would've let loose on them."

Homie lifted his shirt showing me he had a banga, too.

"I feel you but we ain't have no win right then but if I catch 'em slippin'...."

I let the thought sit for a second because I really didn't want to pop a nigga over something I didn't fully understand. This was my first time hearing about having to pay to work on blocks or was this nigga Cash just trying to get over on me.

"We still out here, right?"

"Yeah, but only for a couple mo' days."

They nodded their heads and went back to hustling like ain't shit happen. I went and sat in the van because I knew if April saw me right now, she'll know something was wrong and I ain't feel like talking about it until I figured out what we going to do from here. I knew dude wasn't playing about what he said but I wasn't either. I didn't see his ass out here watching the block or selling bags when it ain't no workers out here so why the fuck he think he going to get some of the money? We had two and a half weeks until the end of the month and the way the weed been moving, we can stack up a little more bread just off that plus what we already had put up we should be good for a while.

My phone rang, breaking my thought. "Hello."

"Baby, where you at?"

"I'm in the back of the van chillin'. Why, what's up?"

"I just was getting ready to go but when I looked out I ain't see you."

"I ain't feel like stayin' in the open."

"Well, I'm about to make these round. You just be careful out there and watch your back."

"Alright, shorty. I'll holla at cha when you get back."

Hanging up, I sat back and thought of everything that led up to this and what I could do next. I shut the block down at one o'clock because I was slipping and on some jumpy shit every time one of the workers came to get another pack.

CHAPTER TWENTY-TWO

"I still don't get why we had to close the weed spot. I know Hectic didn't just stop selling to you for nothing."

"Naw, it wasn't for nothing shit got hot and it gotta cool down so, for now, ain't shit happenin'."

I still haven't told nobody but Hectic what really happen. They all think he cut me off. After I let everybody know we were done, I hit them with a little money just because, then gave the Twins all the weed we had left.

"We don't need him. I can call my uncle and he'll put us back on."

I thought about asking her to holla at her uncle to see what they can do but canceled that out because I ain't have nobody to help run the block since Blacky was still in a coma and I wasn't about to put that much trust in Lil Tone.

It felt good knowing my girl was down for the cause, but I just couldn't do it.

"Man, shorty it's time to chill out for a while. When it's time, then we'll see what's up."

April looked like she wanted to say more about it but said, "So, what's up now?"

"Nothin' really. We just gon' kick it."

"Whatever. What you on today?"

"I was 'bout to hit Lil Tone up and see what he doin'."

I wasn't about to just be sitting in the crib all day and I knew Lil Tone had found something to get into.

"Well, me and Lucky taking the kids out."

"Don't get too comfortable with playin' that mommy shit."

"Why? You don't want no Lil Bishops running around?"

I was only playing but I could tell she was serious.

To be on the safe side I said, "Yeah, one day when the time is right."

"Okay, 'Mr. When The Time Is Right,' think about that when you hitting this next time 'cause you sho' ain't been wearing no condom or pulling out and the last time I checked that's the quickest way to making a baby."

"Alright, I'll get some condoms before I come home."

She just looked at me and didn't say shit, so I picked up the phone and called Lil Tone.

He answered quicker than usual. "Man, what you on?"

"That's what I'm tryin' to ask you. I'm tryin' to get out the crib."

"Shit, I was gon' go get some bread but we can catch up with some hoes. You down?"

"Naw, I wasn't on that but we can go make a lil' money and chill though."

"Alright, I been workin' packs on a few joints. We'll see which one slammin'."

"That's what's up. I'll be at yo crib in a lil' bit."

"Naw, I'm comin' that way anyways so I'll scoop you up."

It's been almost three weeks and we been "joint hopping" where we went to whatever block that we could make the most money on just about every day. The days I missed were to go see Blacky who woke up but couldn't talk or move, yet. Lucky didn't want to leave him now that he was awake, we had to pretty much drag her home the first few days. Now, as long as we got her there first thing in the morning, she was cool until we came to get her at night.

Every day that I went up there I told him what's been happening and tried my best to figure out if he knew who shot him but he just looked at me. I knew he knew and was trying his best to talk so he can tell me.

It wasn't shit for me to do after dropping Lucky off at the hospital so I drove to the block we worked the most, looking for Lil Tone but he wasn't there so I drove to the others but still couldn't find him, so I called him.

"Yeah?" He said, picking up the phone.

"Man, where you at? I been lookin' for yo ass everywhere."

"I'm on the Avenue. I just got out here."

"Yeah, that's the second spot I hit but I'm on my way back now."

"I'll be out here."

I had to turn around but was only about fifteen minutes away. When I got to the Ave, something told me to go down the alley, especially since I ain't see Lil Tone out there with everybody else. As soon as I turned in the alley between Hamlin and Ridgeway, I saw Lil Tone standing behind a garbage can. I thought he was pissing so I stopped and waited but when I looked, I saw that he had a bitch back there bent over fucking the shit out of her. I start busting up laughing and drove up on him.

"Is it good?"

He looked up and start smiling when he saw it was me, then said, "What's good bruh? You want some of this hoe?"

"Man, get yo crazy ass in the back before somebody else ride up."

I thought he was tricking off with a clucka, but when I saw her, shorty was bad.

They got in and I said, "Shorty, what that head be like?"

She popped her lips. "You gotta find out for yo'self."

I just shook my head and went to park the van before I jumped in the back and turned one of the second-row seats around so I can face the bed in the back where Lil Tone was hitting Shorty doggie style. I leaned the seat back and pulled dummy out. Shorty held on to the sides of my seat and start knocking a nigga down something serious. I tried to hold back, but shorty knew what she was doing so it didn't take long before I busted all in her mouth. She tried to drink it all and the little that got away running down my dick she licked it up, making sure she ain't miss a drop.

She sucked on dummy until I went soft again, then moved back, all while Lil Tone was still fucking her. I grabbed some baby wipes and cleaned myself off before getting back behind the wheel. It was about five minutes before they finished with their business and cleaned up.

I turned to shorty as Lil Tone got in the front and asked where she wanted to be dropped off at.

"I'm good right here but when can I get up with y'all again?"

I turned to Lil Tone, letting him know shorty on him. "We'll catch up with you in the area," he said.

With that, she got out and started walking up the block.

"Man, you a fuckin' nut, Joe. Yo ass ain't even look up when I drove up. It coulda been anybody."

"Shit, they probably would've wanted some too."

"You stupid, but what's really good?"

"Same shit, just tryin' to chase paper and hoes."

"That's what's up, but you know I can't be out here chasin' no hoe. Let April even think I'm on that, she gon' nut up on both us."

"Hell naw, leave me outta that. I'm not tryin' to get into it with that crazy girl."

I could tell he was really spooked about what April would do and he knows she'll blame him, so I told him like it was.

"She knows all you be doing is chasin' pussy and think you gon' pull me in that shit, so she gon' blame you."

We were out the van and just got on the corner when Lil Tone was about to say something but stopped when a clucka walked up on us, talkin' shit.

"What's up with you sellin' me a bogus bag, nephew?"

I knew he wasn't talkin' to me so I turned to Lil Tone.

"What dude talkin' about?"

"He knows what I'm talkin' about."

"You got me fucked up. I ain't sell you shit bogus, go somewhere with that bullshit."

"I ain't never had a problem over here with these other niggas and I remember who sell me a bag."

"Man, he said he ain't sell you no bogus bag. That's it. Ain't shit else to talk about."

"I just want my money back and I'll be gone, nephew."

I was starting to get mad but I knew that Lil Tone probably did get down on him. "How much you spend?"

"Just a dub."

I pulled my money out and was about to give the clucka his twenty dollars back but Lil Tone stopped me.

"Whatcha doin' bruh?"

"Giving this crackhead a dub so he can get the fuck out my face."

Lil Tone gave me this crazy look before saying, "Bruh, this bitch ass dude callin' me a thief and a lie, don't give his ass shit."

I ain't want to go against my homie in front of anybody so I put my money back up, knowing that it was going to get dude started back up and just as the thought crossed my mind dude swung on Lil Tone hitting his ass in the eye.

"Yo bitch ass!" I watched as they threw they shit up and got ready to fight. Lil Tone said, "You about to get fucked up!" Then went in on him, hitting the clucka like ten times before dude could even get one swing off.

I sat back and watched as they went at it for a little bit but no matter if my homie was winning or not, I wasn't about to sit back and let him fight by himself. So, when dude crackhead ass stood back to regroup, I cracked his ass, putting him on his back pockets with one hit.

He looked up at me shocked and shit before he said, "Damn nephew, this between me and him."

Lil Tone ran up and field goal kicked his ass in the face.

"Man, shut yo punk ass up!"

Dude was laid out and I sat there laughing while Lil Tone bounced dude head off the ground.

"Damn, homie, you gon' kill his ass." One of the little niggas off the block came up and said but didn't do shit to stop Lil Tone.

"Naw, he gon' live this time but he gon' feel it for a few days." He still ain't stop until some other niggas came running up.

"Fuck y'all niggas on, y'all dumb ass gon' make the block hot!"

"Man, this bitch ass nigga runnin' his mouth talkin' about I sold him a dummy bag."

Anybody could see that this nigga was ready to kill something but this nigga was like a brotha to me, and I know he only acted like this because his dumb ass got caught doing some real stupid shit.

One of the dudes that came over sized Lil Tone up before asking him, "Did ya?"

"Nigga, what you mean, did I? Fuck I got to get down on a crackhead for when I'm gon' get his money anyway?"

"Why the fuck you so mad if you ain't do it?"

Lil Tone didn't have shit to say and homie ain't give him time to.

"Nigga, we getting' too much money ova here to be tryin' to make a cheap dolla' or trippin' about the shit."

I could see where this shit was going, so I took that dub back out and dropped it by the clucka, then said, "Man, it ain't shit. Like you said, we gon' get his money anyway, so fuck it."

Someone said the nigga name but I didn't catch it. He was the same nigga still doing the talking. "Man homie, you good to come back ova here but we ain't down with fuckin our customers up, so that shit gotta be chilled out."

"Don't even trip on it, Lord. We gon' bounce for now and holla at y'all tomorrow or something," I said.

"Bet, homie."

We started walking toward my van but when we got away from the rest of the niggas he stopped and turned to me.

"Man, why you give dude that shit?"

"It ain't shit but part of the game. You win some and you lose some and the way you just beat the fuck outta dude, I say you won that one, so don't trip on it."

"Man, I still wouldn't have gave dude shit."

I ain't want to keep going with that shit so I asked him where he parked.

"I got a ride ova here so I need a ride back to the crib unless you just wanna ride and kick it."

"Naw, I'm about to go holla at my freaky lil snow bunny, but come on, I'll drop you off at the crib."

We went and got in the van and I was about to pop some music in so this nigga wouldn't talk me to death, but as soon as he got in, he started.

"Man, what's up with shorty?"

I already know where he was going with that so I started up the van and pulled off before I answered.

"Ain't shit up with her."

"I'm sayin', tho. I thought April was the only female I couldn't hit."

"Shit, I asked her if I can bring you but she said she ain't tryin' to make it a habit of fuckin' with niggas our age."

Which wasn't no lie but if I would've stressed the issue she would've went along like any other hoe.

"Tell her that this dick ain't no minor, for me, alright?"

I busted out laughing and took that time to pop a tape in. Before it started playing, I said, "I gotcha homie, don't even trip."

I'm happy that he ain't try to holla over the music because it was like an hour before I pulled up in front of his crib since I took all the side streets.

I pulled up, turned the music down. "After I finish with this hoe, I'm probably gon' stay in for the night and kick it with April. But, hit me up in the morning and I'll come pick you up."

"Alright homie, that's what's up. Especially since it's back to the way it started and them other niggas out the way. I'll get at cha later."

He gave me some dap and got out, leaving me confused.

It ain't really what he said, but how he said the shit. Like we both knew something. I ain't wanna think no bullshit about my homie before, but with him saying some shit like that, I had to watch him real close now.

Tryin' to move on with my day, I called Amanda to see what's up and she told me that she'll call when she can get a break. I hung up with her and drove around thinking. Corn on my mind, I drove over to his ol' G's crib to see what was up and when she saw it was me, her face lit up.

She told me she don't do nothing but try to find ways to get her baby out that jam. When I asked what they had on him she told me the only thing they telling her right now is they got a CI and that there is the key evidence. That had me thinkin' but my visit was cut short by a call from Amanda. I left, promising that I'll stop by and call more often.

I met her at a hotel by her job and she was her normal freaky self but as we left she told me she could tell I had a lot on my mind because I wasn't into the sex at all. I told her that I'll make it up to her. As I drove home, I thought to holla at April about what Lil Tone said to see if maybe I was overthinking, but when I got home, I went straight to bed.

CHAPTER TWENTY-THREE

"Damn, April, yo ass ain't never got a nigga something ready to eat no mo'. All you wanna do is eat, fuck and sleep. What's good with that, shorty?"

"I don't know, boy, but don't lie on me. I still cook, just no breakfast."

"That's the point. I want you to cook my breakfast."

"Well, if you haven't realized, I been a little sick in the mornings."

"Go to the doctor then."

"I did."

I looked at her to see if she was going to tell me but when she didn't, I just asked, "Alright, what they say?"

She started smiling. "They said we got a baby on the way." When I just looked at her without saying shit, she said, "Baby, I'm pregnant!"

I heard what she said the first time. I just ain't have shit to say, so I turned and walked out the room.

"John, where the fuck you going? I just said that I'm pregnant with yo' damn baby!"

I kept going and grabbed my keys. The last thing I heard before I walked out the crib was her yelling calling me a bitch ass nigga.

I was just about to close the front door but Lucky came up.

"Hey, Bishop."

I just pushed the door open for her and kept walking, got in my van and spun off. I was about to call Lil Tone but realized I forgot to grab my phone and I wasn't about to go back to grab it.

Riding around for a while, I began to think about the time I asked my mama about my pops...

"I was the girl that all the dudes wanted but mainly the bad boys, they'll be running up behind me trying to get my attention, but I wasn't interested in none of them. I was sixteen when this one hustler used to approach me every day. One day I come home and a brand-new car was parked in front of my house and the hustler came and handed me the key, telling me that was for my sixteenth birthday. He said I could get a new car every birthday if I just saved myself for him until my eighteenth birthday, but none of that was appealing to me."

"So, how you meet my pops then and what was so different about him?"

She just sat there with a smile that told me she was thinking about a lot of good times. Moments passed and she looked at me. "Your dad was a good man. He just wasn't man enough to be a father."

"He was the one that didn't come at me. Instead, he waited until the right time to get close to my father. It ain't come for years, it came when I was nineteen and my father's car broke down. He fixed the car and started doing work with my father and they got close and that was when he asked if he can take me out."

She stopped talking and was staring off into space, so I asked, "Okay, so what happened?"

"Nothing really, until about a year later when your grandparents got killed in an accident. He was like the only one there for me when I needed someone and that's how he stole my heart and I gave all of myself to him. We had plans to get married but he wanted a steady job and even though that job stuff ain't mean nothing, I didn't try to rush him because every-thing was perfect with us. When I found out I was pregnant with you, I waited a whole month before I told him because I wanted it to be the right time. One day after he left for work, I made his favorite meal and waited for him to come home. When I saw him coming down the block I put on the Switch album, which was his favorite album of all time.

"When he came in, I knew everything was just going to be even better and when he did a little two-step over to where I was standing, he picked me up, and gave me the sweetest kiss. He put me down and gave me a smile that lit up the room before asking what was the special occa-sion. I had planned to wait util after we ate but that smile changed my plans and I told him then.

'Baby, I'm pregnant!' And as soon as the words left my lips, that smile went away as he told me I better not be. I thought it was his way to hear me say it again, so I put my arm around his neck and whispered that we were having a kid.

"He backed up, just looking at me with a spiteful look that broke my heart before turning his back on us. A coward ass nigga was what I called him, and the last words I said to him.

I heard the pain in her voice and thought she was going to start crying but she turned to me. "John, promise me one thing."

"Okay, mama?"

"Promise that you'll never do what your father did."

"I promise, I won't, mama. I promise."

I held my mama and that was the only time we ever spoke of him. I don't even know what his name was.

———

With the promise I made to my mama and the thought that April was the only person besides her that I loved. I turned around and raced back home. I pulled up and parked. Seeing that April's car was still there, I ran into the crib.

I got to our room and found April in the bed.

"So, yo bitch ass came back, huh? So, what you need? Help packing or is you going to kick me out?"

I could tell that she was just crying because her eyes were red so I knew she was just acting tough. I sat next to her and tried to pull her close to me but she pulled away and went to the other side of the bed.

"Alright, shorty, I guess I had that comin' but you just told me that we got a baby on the way and look how we livin'. Every time we leave the house it's a chance that we can get popped and sent back to somebody else's house away from each other."

"You gotta come better than that 'cause that shit was weak as hell."

"Shorty, I'm scared."

She looked at me like I was playing but asked, "Of what?"

"Of being a nothing like my father. Of not being able to give y'all everything y'all want. You want me to keep goin'?"

"You ain't in this shit by yourself and whenever you ready to stop workin' packs I'm sure we can get shit back to moving like it was before and if you ain't realize we got a nice amount of money put up that we can live good off of for a while."

I had a million thoughts running through my mind and kind of spaced out until April came back over and hugged me.

I looked her in the eyes. "Give me some time to holla at Corn and Hectic, we gon' get shit back the way it needs to be but I need you, Shorty, 'cause this shit ain't easy to do by myself."

"Baby, you should already know I got you. So, what you want to have, a boy?"

"Naw, I want a little girl so she can be just like her mama. Speakin' of that, we need to have Ms. Kelly set up a doctor's appointment so our baby comes out healthy."

For the next three days, we didn't leave the crib or answer the phones or the door. We just talked about everything we wanted to do for our baby. I swear I felt like we planned the next eighteen years. I finally told her everything about my family and she understood my fear of following in my father's footsteps. She told me some stuff about her parents I didn't know and told me that she wanted to start writing them again so they can stop worrying and let them know they were going to have a grandbaby.

The first person we went to see was Ms. Kelly about the doctor appointments and to get us up to see Corn. Ms. Kelly was the motherly type. Mixed, she was light-skinned, a short, robust woman with long, straight hair. She was happy about the baby and made us promise that every time that we needed a babysitter, we'll come to her. She said it would be about a month before we can go visit Corn but it'll happen.

Leaving her house, we went to check on Lucky and drop her off some money. We got good news, Blacky should be home from the hospital next week and taking a speech class because his throat swelled up and fucked up his speech.

I told her we were going to throw a little party for him but she said to put that on hold. They didn't want anybody to know he was coming home until he was back on his feet.

April let her know that we were having a baby and when they got to talking about that it was no stopping them. I started playing with the kids until they were finished talking. Before we left, Lucky told us that she wanted us to be there when Blacky got released from the hospital and it wouldn't be no other way.

CHAPTER TWENTY-FOUR

It only took a little over two weeks for us to get approved to visit Corn but so much other shit was going on that we planned to go at the end of the month. I only kicked it with Blacky on the day he came home. He was spaced out. I told him to hit me up when he was ready and he just nodded. Lucky called every day and told us how he doing.

"Man, you good?" Lil Tone was waving his hand in my face.

I was on the block with Lil Tone just chillin' while he worked packs.

"Yeah, I'm straight. What's good?"

"I said you gon' let me be the godfather for your baby, right?"

"Oh, I ain't even hear you but you already know you gonna be the godfather. Nigga, I'm surprised yo ass ain't pop one of the bust downs, yet."

"Hell naw, I be strappin' up with them hoes. I ain't with that baby mama shit."

He finished what he was saying but started to focus on four cars riding down the block. I looked and all the cars were niggas that be on this block so I didn't pay it much attention.

"Man, I'm not tryin' to play her like that but it's more to..."

I didn't finish my sentence because I could tell that they were on some bullshit. Buddy Lord, a dark skin, six-foot stocky nigga with brown eyes and a bald head was in the lead car. He had it for the block. He pulled curbside in a grey Cadillac and hopped out. The closer he got I could see the red 5-point star located on his left temple. "Didn't I tell yo bitch ass to stay the fuck off my block?"

"That shit was bogus, Big Homie. I ain't sell that shit to dude."

Behind him, a blue Regal, a red Cutlass and a burgundy Park Avenue pulled curbside. Two got out of one, three got out the next and one got out the other, the driver in its front seat smoking a blunt and looking on as they prepared to do whatever. The five of them surrounded us and I got a bad feeling.

Buddy Lord stroked his full beard in frustration. "I ain't even tryin' to hear that shit. How much money you got on you, bitch nigga?"

He didn't even wait for an answer. He went in Lil Tone's pockets and took his money and work, then started laughing.

"So, you just gonna serve yo own shit on my block?" He looked Lil Tone up and down, then turned to me. "What about you, you serving too?"

"I ain't got shit to do with that, homie."

"You out here with dude, so you got a lot to do with it. Now, how much you got on you?"

He went to reach for my pockets but I stepped back.

"That's what you on?"

He up'd his banga so I gave him what I had on me. I wasn't trying to get shot over five-hundred dollars.

"Man, you bogus, but it ain't shit."

"That's what I'm talking about. Charge that shit to the game and while you at it, put this ass whoppin' on it too."

I was about to throw my guard up to fight him but some nigga hit me from behind. The next thing I knew it was like four niggas hitting me and I went down. I tried to cover my face but they got a few hits off. I could feel the blood running down my face.

Finally, they stopped and dude came over to me.

"If I ever catch y'all over here again, I'm gon' have one of these niggas put some hot shit in y'all dumb ass."

I stood up and just looked at him. I had my banga in the van, I just needed to get to it.

"Hurry up and get off my block before we do it now."

Lil Tone was still on the ground fucked up, so I helped him up and we walked to the van.

We hopped in the van, and Lil Tone wiped his face. "Man bro, I'm sorry, I fucked up."

It wasn't shit he could say that was going to make this go away but it wasn't the time for that. "Fuck that shit. I'm about to shoot this bitch up. Get in."

I hopped in on the driver's side and got my gun from under the seat and checked it to make sure the safety was off.

"I ain't even bring my shit with me."

"It don't matter. This gon' do the trick for now. I'm coming back."

"I'm with you then."

I started the van and pulled it in the middle of the street before I got out. Them niggas was still standing at the corner so I ran on the sidewalk and before they could up their bangas or run, I start letting off

Boom! Boom! Boom!

I didn't stop until I emptied the clip. I saw I hit at least two, but I wasn't about to stay around to see if I shot more. I ran back to the van and peeled off.

When we were a few blocks away, I looked at Lil Tone and wanted to slap the shit out of him with my banga. "Fuck! What kind of bitch shit was that? You had me over there bogus and ain't tell me shit!"

"Man, I'm sorry."

"That sorry shit ain't about nothing, nigga. I still got a busted head and lost my money for some bullshit. I got a shorty on the way and them niggas could've just killed a nigga."

"But you just fucked they bitch ass up and we going back again."

The nigga was smiling like the shit was funny. I snapped. "Nigga, now if one of them niggas die, I'm going to jail 'cause you got me caught up in yo dumb shit, tryin' to make a cheap dolla. Man, if you wasn't already fucked up, I'd pull over and beat yo ass."

I wanted him to say something, just so I can slap the shit out of him, but he just sat there looking stupid.

I had to get out this van and Lil Tone's crib was closer, so I called April.

"Hello."

"Baby, I need you to come pick me up from Lil Tone's crib."

"What's wrong?"

"We'll talk about it later."

"Okay baby, just be careful."

I hung up and tried to stay focused and make it to Lil Tone's crib, but every time I saw a police car I got nervous, a few times damn near hitting something.

By the time I pulled up in front of his crib, I could barely keep my hands from shaking. I got out and walked to the corner so I wouldn't do nothing to Lil Tone but he walked up behind me.

"Man, I know you mad and I know I fucked up, but we brothas, man. That shit ain't about nothing we gon..."

"Nigga, you ain't even making no sense right now and whatever you was about to say, *we* ain't gon' do shit."

"Alright. I see what's up but I guess I had that coming. Just know that if you need me, I'm here."

He just stood there but I ain't have shit else to say to him. He finally walked off when my phone rang and I still didn't say shit.

"What's good?"

"I'm about to pull up. Where you at?"

"I'm right on the corner."

"Oh, I see you."

She hung up and a few seconds later, pulled up. I got in and when she saw my face and the blood all over my shirt, she went crazy.

"What the fuck happened, John? Is that all your blood?"

Before I could answer, she said, "I swear, I knew Lil Tone was going to get you involved in some bullshit."

I didn't know if she was done, so I didn't say nothing which made her yell.

"Boy, what the fuck happened? You okay? Tell me something!"

"Yeah, I'm good."

"So, what happened?"

"I was chillin' with Lil Tone goofy ass on 15th and Ridgeway and the niggas from over there jumped us 'cause this nigga was sellin' dummy bags and they told him he can't serve over there."

"Okay, what that got to do with you? You was serving too?"

"Naw, I was just kickin' it with the nigga but they wasn't tryin' to hear that shit. Them niggas took my money and beat my ass."

"You should go beat his ass."

"I wanted to but he already fucked up bad but I ain't got shit else to say to him."

"Okay, so, what's wrong with the van?"

"Ain't shit wrong with it. I just didn't know if they told the police what I was drivin'."

"Bishop, what did you do?"

"What the fuck you mean, 'What did I do?' Them bitch ass niggas jumped me, put they feet on me, so I shot their block up and hit a couple of them."

"Well, it is what it is, but until we get this shit back going you ain't going nowhere without me."

"Yes, ma'am, whatever you say."

We drove off and went straight home.

April took care of me, making sure I wouldn't be too swelled up. The next morning, I was too sore to move. We caught the WGN news, they said that two niggas got murdered and two got shot and released from the hospital. They said the police are investigating but that it appears to be drug-related.

I must have got lost in my thoughts, staring off into space because I damn near jumped out of my skin when April sat next to me and then touched me.

She looked me in the eyes, "Baby, you did what you had to do, so don't trip over it."

"Yeah, I know, but it was over some dumb ass shit."

"That was still on them."

I just shook my head and went back to my thoughts deciding shit had to change from this point on.

CHAPTER TWENTY-FIVE

It was finally the day for us to go holla at Corn. Since the shooting, we only left the crib yesterday to go to the doctor about the baby. They told us that she was two months and we can find out if it was a boy or girl soon but we wanted it to be a surprise. We spent most of the night talking about names. April told me she wanted our girl to have her middle name; Jasmine and that was my mama's name. If we had a girl her name will be Jasmine Elise Thompson and if it was a boy then he'll be my Jr.

I got dressed before I woke April up, then went to my book to see how much money we had saved up and how much we'll be able to spend. We still had most of everything we made. I told myself that we'll start having some fun with it instead of just stacking it.

I was sitting in the front room when it was a knock on the door. I went and looked out the window and saw Ms. Kelly.

I opened the door. "I thought you was coming at ten-thirty?"

"Hi to you, too."

"My fault, how you doing?" I hugged her and let her in.

"I thought I'll come a little early so we can have a little talk before we go."

"Alright, let me go see if April is ready."

I went to the room and found April putting her hair up in a ponytail.

"Baby, Ms. Kelly here and wanna holla at us about something."

"I'm almost done. Just give me a minute."

"Alright."

I walked back to the living room. "You want something to drink?" I asked Ms. Kelly.

"Some water, if you can."

"Yeah, we got bottled water."

"That's good."

I went to get me and April a juice and Ms. Kelly's water.

While I got it, Ms. Kelly said loud enough for me to hear, "I like how y'all keep the place clean. I didn't expect it to be this nice."

Coming back in the living room I said, "That's all April's work. If she see any dirt she cleaning the whole room, but thank you... we want it to be clean like when we moved in."

I handed her the water, then sat on the couch.

April came in the room. "Hey, Mama Kelly."

"It's about to be Grandma Kelly. How you doing, baby?"

"Good. Just trying to keep this boy out of trouble."

"Girl, you fighting a losing battle because boys going to be boys until they get in some kind of jam."

"What's up, though? Don't y'all see me sittin', right here? At least wait until I'm not around or something. But can we talk about what you gotta holla at us about 'cause I'm trying to stop and get some breakfast."

"Baby, I'm sorry I forgot you were here."

Me and her got real close in the last couple of weeks so I could tell that she was being sarcastic, but then she switched up real quick and got down to business.

"Y'all trying to get back in the game, right?"

I just nodded my head, not knowing where she was going.

"Well, it's a lot more to it than just copping the shit and having dudes on the block selling it. Y'all gotta be ready to do it all now and it's not going to be no stop and go stuff. Once you out, you out."

"We in it now. We ain't stoppin'."

"That conversation is for another day but unless you want it to end in a cage or box, you'll plan an out because it will end, I bet my last dollar on that. What all y'all trying to put out there?"

I looked at April, back at Mama Kelly, and shrugged. "The weed and rocks like before, I guess."

"You got your own connect with the weed, right?"

"Yeah."

"And y'all still plan to be on this block?"

"Yeah, but we tryin' to get more blocks and still keep all the weed spots we had."

"I'll let Corn deal with all that but as far as y'all still staying here, I don't like it so I want y'all to move in one of my houses. The only thing is, y'all can't have nobody coming over there."

April was sitting back listening but speaking up, she said, "But we need the twins to come over and help bag the stuff up, and what about Blacky and Lucky?"

"Y'all can have this apartment to do the dirt out of but the house is where you lay your head at and the way y'all about to get on, y'all don't want too many people knowing where that is." She paused for a second, then said, "If y'all sure that y'all can trust them, then do what you do, but remember that money changes people and it'll turn a real nigga, fake."

"Alright, that's cool. I'll let y'all handle all that but we ain't moving nothin' out of here 'cause I want all new stuff, especially for my baby's room," April said.

"That's all good with me. Now, the last thing is when you talking to Corn don't say nothing about drugs. He'll tell you everything you need to know."

"Alright, but can we go now? I know my baby is hungry."

"I know I am but this one in here probably don't know about that," April said, rubbing her belly that was still flat which I had to say something about.

"I can't wait until yo stomach starts getting fat."

"Girl, you better be happy that he want to see you when you get like that. Most of 'em don't even want to sleep with you no more when you get big."

I smiled. "You can't tell her nothin'."

"Don't make me go upside yo head, boy."

"Alright, let's go get her some food before she get violent."

It was May, so we still were wearing jackets, once we were all ready and leaving out the door I asked April where did she want to eat at.

"I want some Church's."

"Hell, naw, shorty, ain't nobody tryin' to eat no chicken this early."

"Oh, this early in the process. Wait a couple more months. She goin' to have you goin' to crazy places in the middle of the night for some crazy ass food. Boy, you probably goin' to be eating pizza and ice cream with her."

"Yeah whatever, y'all win."

We hit the Church's up on Madison and ordered take out, then ate on the way downtown to the Feds holding. When we got there, it was a whole bunch of shit that we had to go through just to get inside since it was a contact visit that Corn's lawyer set up. After getting stripped searched we sat in the visiting room for half an hour just waiting.

As soon as he stepped in the room, I could tell he had a lot on his mind but he smiled when he saw us. "Man, there go my Lil nigga. What's good with it, homie?"

I got up and hugged him. "Shit, just chillin, man. Joe, I been on ten since I knew we can come up here."

He looked at April. "Come give yo big bro a hug." She did and he said, "I heard I'm about to be an uncle."

"Yeah, but this big head boy almost missed out on being a daddy."

"Oh, I guess it's my turn now since yo friends come first and mama come last, huh?" Mama Kelly joked with open arms.

"Now you know I gotta save the best for last." He hugged and kissed his mama then said to us, "Y'all know I gotta make her feel important."

Ms. Kelly hit him in the chest, "Get yo hands off me. I know I'm important!"

We all laughed and sat down. It got quiet like nobody could find nothing to say, so I spoke up. "Man, what's been up with you?"

"It's crazy man, these people ain't playin' fair. They tryin' to send a nigga up the river on some bullshit but I don't wanna talk about that right now. What's goin' on out there?"

"Man, it ain't the same without you. I'm talking about Blacky been out the hospital a minute now but he ain't come out the crib and messin' with Lil Tone, I got robbed and jumped by some niggas."

I wanted to tell him how I got down on the niggas but if he didn't wanna talk about the drugs I wasn't about to talk about no murders.

"Man homie, you can't let yoself get caught up in stupid situations like that. And now you got so much to lose, you can't be out there like that with niggas that's not on the same shit you on."

"Yeah, I feel that but what you be on in here?"

We sat back and he told us about how he just be spending his days working out and reading every law book he can get his hands on. He told me how mail be the only thing that makes the day better.

"So, you gon' be some kinda lawyer or something when you get outta here?"

"I don't know about all that, but I'm gon' try something new."

"What's up? You want me to get some female to write you?"

"That'll be what's up but y'all send enough mail and pictures to let a nigga know he loved."

The officer stepped into the room.

"Mr. Kelly, ten minutes. Start wrapping it up."

"Damn, it seem like y'all just got here, but I'm happy I got to see y'all."

"We going to have to come back because somebody wanted to take over the whole conversation," April said, then looked at me.

"Ay, check it, though. I know the business and I can make it happen but it's something that gotta be taken care of 'cause I ain't tryin' to have you go down like me, especially by the same CI."

"Alright, whoever it is, just tell me and I'll..."

"Naw, naw. We ain't on that but I know you smart enough to figure it out. And when the time is right everything will be in order."

"Okay, Mr. Kelly, your visit is over. Give your family a quick hug and let's go."

He didn't leave out the room this time but just stood there.

I was kind of lost in my thoughts, trying to figure out what he was saying until he hit me on the shoulder.

I zoned back in and shook it off. "What's up?"

"Nigga, get up and give me a hug."

I looked and saw everybody waiting on me, so I got up and gave him a brotherly hug.

"Man, keep yo head up in here."

"You do the same out there and keep yo eyes open, too."

I was expecting him to say more but when he just walked off, I was even more confused.

I waited until we were in the car before I asked Ms. Kelly did she know what he was talking about.

"I know, but he wants you to figure it out yourself."

"How I'ma do that and I don't know shit about shit."

"When it's right it'll come to you and when it does, you'll know. Just think about it."

I ain't have nothing else to say because I could tell that I wasn't going to get nothing out of her, so I sat back and thought about it the rest of the ride.

At home, I asked April the same thing.

"I'm confused too, baby," she said. "I don't know why they won't just tell us what they talking about."

"Fuck it. I'll figure it out one way or the other."

We left it at that and went about the rest of our day.

CHAPTER TWENTY-SIX

"Boy, don't you hear yo phone ringing?"

Me and April were just coming from the store, buying new furniture and other shit for the new crib.

"Naw, I was just in a daze."

I looked at the caller ID and saw that it was Amanda. I wanted to ignore her call but I've been giving her the spin around for the last three weeks so I answered it.

"Yeah, what's up?"

I put the phone to my ear, away from April, so she couldn't hear who I was talking to.

"Can we meet up today?"

"I'm kinda busy with my girl right now."

"John, you been busy for a month now and it's getting old, so can we please meet now?"

I know I could've just changed my number and be done with shorty but I want to keep my word or at least holla at her in person.

I wanted to spend the day with April so I told Amanda to hold on and asked April, "You cool if I drop you off at the crib and go holla at somebody?"

"I don't care. I need some sleep anyway. Who is it anyway?"

"It's a business deal I made but we'll talk about it later."

"Do what you do."

Talking back in the phone I said, "I gotta drop my girl off, then I'll hit you back."

"Okay, just hurry up."

I hung up and thought about how I was going to explain to her that we had to end that shit and still have her help me if I got caught up. Then I had to find out how I was going to tell April.

When we got to the crib April turned to me. "Baby, you need to get rid of this van."

I looked at her like she was crazy. "Fuck, I'ma do that for?"

"Because the niggas could be looking for you or they could've told the police what you was driving."

"Yeah, I'll holla at Ms. Kelly about that."

"What time you think you'll be back?"

"I don't even know, but I'll try to be fast."

"Naw, it's cool. Just call so I can tell you what I want to eat."

"Alright, baby. I'll talk to you when I get back."

I leaned over and kissed her before she got out and I waited until she got in the house before I pulled off.

The last few times that I got up with Amanda it was at her house so I didn't even call to ask where she wanted to meet at. She lived by the White Sox stadium neighborhood so it was a good twenty minutes to get there.

I pulled into the driveway and parked beside her car.

Hopping out and closing the door behind me, I thought about using the key she gave me but, instead, I rang the doorbell.

I saw her shadow before she asked, "Who is it?"

"It's me. Open the door."

When she opened the door and saw me standing there she said, "I thought you were going to call me. What happened? And why didn't you use your key?"

She was all happy and shit but when she looked at me, she asked, "What's wrong, baby? Did I do something wrong?"

"I got to holla at you, but naw, you ain't do shit."

"Come in, then. We can talk in the room."

I followed her to her room. I tried not to get turned on at the way her ass was bouncing in the shorts she was wearing but it was like my dick had a mind of its own.

We got in the room, she jumped on the bed, and when I sat down, she came rubbing on my shoulders. "Now, tell me what's wrong."

I still didn't know how to tell her, so I just said what it was. "My girl pregnant."

"Is it April?"

"Yeah."

"Well at least she ain't ugly, but anyway, I know where this going but you still have to be in your kid's life."

"That goes without saying. It's the thing with us that…"

I didn't' want to say it was a problem so I just let the sentence hang in the air.

"I know you want to end the thing we got going on, right?"

"Yeah, but I don't want you to think I'm not keeping my word."

"I got that, John, but what I'm saying is you have to take care of your kid that you having by me, too, because I'm pregnant."

I heard what she said but I had to make sure. "Whatcha say?"

"You got me pregnant, too."

I didn't want to act like I did with April but I couldn't just accept this so I asked, "You wasn't fucking nobody else?"

She looked at me for a second before answering. "Yeah, it was a few other guys if you must know but I made all of them wear condoms."

I jumped up out the bed. "I'll be there for my kid but this shit still over with."

"Can we do it one more time, please?"

"I'm good."

She grabbed me by the shirt and pulled me back in the bed.

"This last time and I promise I'll still help you if you be in our baby's life."

I laid back. "Just give me some head."

Without hesitation, she started pulling my pants off, then taking dummy out the boxers.

She looked me in the eyes as she played with it before she took it all down her throat.

"I don't know what you did to me but I'm going to miss our time together."

Like always, she laid her best head game on me.

Every time I got close to nutting, she'll stop, leaving me with the feeling that I busted.

After the third time of her doing that, I couldn't take it no more, so I pushed her on her back and rolled her shorts off. Her pussy was dripping wet. I went down and tasted her juices for the last time.

I came up. "Yeah, I gonna miss it too, shorty."

Giving her my full length on the first stroke, I slowly made love to my soon-to-be child's mama. I savored the moment as long as I could but with her wetness and her working her pussy muscles I came so hard that it start seeping out of her. I let her ride her waves through, got up and went to the bathroom to freshen up. Clean now, I left, leaving the spare key on the kitchen table.

I drove straight home, but when I got there I wasn't able to face April, yet. So, I just kept riding around the block. I started to go to the square house to holla at Pops but when I parked and got out the van, I just walked to the crib.

It was quiet and dark, except for the night lights that April kept in the kitchen and the hallway. I went in the bedroom to find April sleeping in one of my white T's with nothing else on. I sat on the bed and just watched her sleep.

After a few minutes without warning, she said, "My mama and daddy told me what it was like, and both of them said that it's part of the game. Hoes was throwing pussy at my daddy and he wasn't always able to turn it down. My mama said she accepted it as long as it wasn't none of her friends or enemies and didn't no kids come of it. She said that as a woman she couldn't go out there fucking because she had too much respect for herself, so that's what I'm going to do."

"My daddy told me that even though he fucked them females and my mama knew, he made sure he didn't put it out there for all to see. But the most important thing he said was that he only loved my mama and that he'll never let no female come between his family or money, and that's what I want you to always remember and do."

Her eyes had been closed the whole time and when I didn't say anything, she opened them and looked at me. "Where you fuck up at?"

I waited a second before saying, "She's pregnant."

"I really don't want to talk about it but it better not be Mrs. Devil as you call her and it better not happen again. Now, let's go to sleep and we'll talk in the morning."

I took my clothes off and laid next to her and watched as she fell back to sleep. I knew sleep wasn't going to happen, so I just sat up and thought about everything that's been going on but none of it made sense. I kept switching from thought to thought. It was a long night but right before the sun began to rise, I got up and took a shower, then went and made some pancakes, bacon and eggs for breakfast.

I walked in the room with the food. April sat up. "Normally, when my daddy fucked up, he bought Mama some diamonds or something that cost a lot of money, but I guess I'll take breakfast in bed."

I sat it down and she said, "She must be ugly as hell or that bitch. Which one?" When I ain't say shit, she snapped. "Boy, just tell me who it is!"

"My caseworker."

She laughed. "A white girl?" She laughed again, then after a quick pause she said, "Oh, that's how you got away when you got arrested, huh?"

"Yeah, I made a deal with her that I'll kick it with her every other week but I shut that down last night."

"Boy, you going to be in that kid life and my baby going to spend time with her brother or sister."

"Yeah, I know."

"I came home early the day she taught you everything and I watched as you gave my dick to that bitch... Ms. Davis."

It wasn't nothing I could say so I just sat there watching her eat.

When she was done she said, "We should go back to the Davis's one day."

"That's what you wanna do? Then we'll go."

"I never told nobody but he tried to rape me."

"Get the fuck outta here. When that happen?"

"It was before you came. He came in my room one night and started touching me, then pulled out his thing and tried to make me give him head. I had my knife and that was the only thing that stopped him."

"I swear on my mama's grave, I'll kill that dude!"

I was heated and ready to get at dude right then and when my phone rang, I snatched it off the dresser.

"What?!"

"Man, homie, I need you to spin on me."

"Who the fuck is this?"

"It's Blacky, you cool homie?"

"Blacky! Nigga, my bad. I just got some fucked up news but what's up?"

I pointed at the phone and mouthed, "Blacky" to April.

"I need to holla at cha, Joe."

"Alright. I'll be over there as soon as I can."

I hung up the phone without even saying "Bye" because I was so charged up.

"What he say, baby?"

"He wants me to come holla at him."

"How he sound?"

"He sounded like he always did."

"Shit, we'll finish this talk later. Let me get dressed."

CHAPTER TWENTY-SEVEN

"What's up, Lucky?"

"Nothing, just doing me."

After I got Blacky's call, I went through like three lights trying to get here.

"What's up, Bishop?" It was Blacky's lil boy.

"What's up with cha, lil man?"

"Nothing. I told Mommy and Daddy that Lil Man is my new name because that's what you call me."

"Okay, Lil Man, where yo daddy at anyways?"

"He in his room."

"Alright. I need to go holla at him, give me some."

After he slapped me five, I told April and Lucky to let me holla at him by myself.

"That's what he wanted anyways."

I nodded my head and went back to the room. Blacky was sitting on his bed, smoking a blunt.

"What's good with it, nigga?"

"Shit, just been spending time with the family."

He got up and hugged me.

"Man, I really appreciate you takin' care of them when I was down, real talk."

"Homie, that ain't shit, but what I need to know is who got down on you cause he dead."

Blacky just looked at me. Taking a long pull, he narrowed his eyes as he exhaled a thick cloud of smoke. "You sure about that?"

"Hell yeah, nigga, I'm sure. If you know who it is and we catch the bitch nigga, I swear on my mama's grave that nigga dead."

"It was Lil Tone."

For some reason, I wasn't surprised. I almost expected him to say that and now that he had, shit was falling into place. "Man, you sure?"

"I was out there by myself for about ten minutes before he came. He stayed on until the little rush was over. I saw him creep off and the next thing I knew he come in the gangway masked up and shot me. I felt him take all the money and the rest of the work. Before he shot me again, he said I wasn't taking his spot."

"That's some bitch shit. Why you ain't tell me before?"

"Truthfully, I didn't know if I could trust you, being dude was yo homie. But you showed me you was a real nigga."

"Well, I know now and that nigga time is about to run out."

"I just need you to set him up. I wanna smoke his hoe ass."

"That goes without saying."

I told him what we were on and he was down with it. We kicked it for another twenty minutes before April and Lucky came busting in.

"Dang, Bishop. Can somebody else talk to him?"

She came to the bed and hugged Blacky.

"What's up, Ms. Crazy?"

"If I'm crazy it's because of him." April pointed at me, sat down next to him and asked, "So, how you doing?"

"I'm good. Shit, ain't no little bullet gon' stop me."

Still standing in the doorway Lucky said, "Yo ass talkin' that shit now. Don't let it happen again or I'm gon' to knock yo ass out that coma just to fuck you up."

I started laughing but April cut it short.

"The same go for you, so you can stop all that laughing, boy."

"Well, we done talkin our business now and since I ain't sleep all night thinkin' about that, I'm about to go to sleep, so I'll holla at y'all later."

"Man, I still got yo banga. You want it back?"

"Damn, I was wonderin' what happened to it. Hell yeah, I want my baby back."

We said our goodbyes and me and April left.

We were halfway home before April asked about what he said.

"He said that Lil Tone was the one that got down on him."

"Ooh, ooh, that's what it is!"

"What?" I asked, confused as hell.

"That's who Corn was talking about baby. Lil Tone tricked on him."

I thought about it and it all made sense now.

"Fuck. I should've never brought this bitch ass nigga out here, man. All the shit I did for his bitch ass."

"Baby, don't even stress on it because we know now and he got his coming."

"Still, he was supposed to be my brotha and he pulled two

bitch ass moves that could've fuck up what I had going on. Now, I gotta play it cool to get him."

"One of my daddy's favorite sayings was, 'You gotta play a sucka to catch a sucka, and really all you gotta do is wave a little pussy in that nigga face and he goin."

"Yeah, I'm gonna holla at him right after we move, but fuck that nigga until then."

It was easier said than done because for the next week all I could think about was his bitch ass.

————

"Hey, baby! I ain't seen you in a long time. Give me a hug."

"What's up, Mama T?"

"What you been up to?"

"Nothing much, just rippin' and runnin', tryin' to do me. You know we about to have a baby, right?"

"Naw, boy, Tone ain't tell me that."

"Yeah, April a few months in."

"Well, at least you got a good girl, but I know you ain't come here to talk to an old lady, so you can go on back."

It was easy talking to Mama T but walking to Lil Tone's room I had to work to be able to smile. It took everything in me not to go in on him when I saw him.

"What's good, my nigga?"

"I ain't on shit. Just came through to see what's up with you."

"You know me. I'm just a squirrel tryin' to get a nut."

"Still chasin' pussy, huh?"

"Yeah, man, but check it, bro, that's my bad on what happened that day. I should've thought before takin' you over there."

"Fuck that shit, homie. It's over with now."

"What's up with yo boy, Blacky?"

I had to catch myself from doin' his ass in right there. It took everything in me to say, "That nigga a hoe, man. I don't even talk to his bitch ass no more."

"So, I can shoot my shot at his girl?"

April told me that he'll set himself up and I was waiting for him to say something like that.

"His girl? Nigga, how you gon' cut me out the picture. That's our girl."

"Yeah?"

"Hell yeah. I've been blowin' that bitch back out every chance I get."

"Bro, that's crazy. You been holdin' out on yo boy like that."

"Don't even trip. I got you."

I gave it a second, like it was a second thought, before I said, "You know what, let me go handle some business. Then we can bust her down tonight."

"Nigga, stop playin'."

"I'm for real. Let me spin and handle this. Be at my crib in an hour."

"Bro, you that nigga."

"Something like that."

I got up and gave him some dap before walking out.

Mama T came out her room when I walked past.

"Don't be takin' so long coming over here no mo' and when you do, you better bring me some of that good ass weed."

"Don't trip. I got you."

"Well, you be safe out there, honey."

"Alright. I'll holla at you Mama T."

I got outside and practically ran to the car and called April.

"Hello."

"Baby, check it out. I need you to call Blacky and have him find a crack head female and have them go to that motel in Riverdale."

"Slow down Bishop, what are you talking about?"

"Baby, I got Lil Tone bitch ass thinkin' he gon' fuck Lucky and we need somewhere to take him and that's a low-key spot."

"Why didn't you just call him yo'self?"

"I don't even know, but do that for me."

"I got you, baby. Where you at now?"

"Outside his crib about to come home."

"Okay, I'll see you then. Love you."

"Love you, too."

I just sat there and thought about how shit was going to be back to the way it should be, for the most part. All that'll be missin' is Corn. When I was pullin' off, I thought of one more thing and called Lil Tone.

"Yo?"

"Ay, homie, don't tell nobody you gon' be with me, 'cause April gon' know we on something if we together."

"That cool, homie."

"I'll holla in a lil' bit."

"Bet."

I hung up, drove home and I barely got in before April was on me.

"Boy, I hope you ain't jump the gun and showed that nigga your hand."

"Naw, baby. He just fell into it his damn self."

I told her how it went and she said, "I guess he is blind to everything when he thinking about pussy."

"Which is all the time."

We got a good laugh at Lil Tone's expense.

"What now?"

"You handled that business."

"Yeah, he said he was going to call when everything is set up."

"Shit, let's chill, then."

We sat around talking about anything and everything, wasting time until Blacky called.

"Man Bishop, what you want me to do, now?"

"Just lay low. I'll call you when we almost there."

"What about this clucka?"

"You ain't let the people at the desk see you, right?"

"Naw, I sent her in."

"Alright, give her a hundred and send her about her way."

There was a knock on the door.

"Dude at my door now. I'll holla at you in a lil bit.

I got up to let him in.

"Don't let him in." April screwed her face up. "I don't want my house to be infested with no rat."

"If you can't play it cool for a few minutes, then go in the room."

Without a word, she got up and went to the back. I opened the door and let Lil Tone in.

"What's happenin'?"

"You."

"April here?"

"Yeah, she in the back sleeping."

"No, I'm not. I'm going with ya'll."

"April, I won't get him in no trouble."

"I know you won't because I'm coming too."

"Baby, we on something. Chill."

"What? Y'all about to go fuck some bitch? I don't care. Shit, this pussy stay wet now, too, so I don't even think y'all and the hoes y'all about to fuck can keep up with me."

"April, you just don't know. I'll hit that shit like it never been hit."

The way Lil Tone was looking made me feel all the more justified about what was about to take place. And though I knew April was just talking, the shit Lil Tone said made me wanna beat the fuck outta him.

April looked back as though she was thinking about it and shrugged. "I don't know about that, but we'll have to see."

"Shit, we ain't gotta go nowhere to find that out."

"Yeah, we do. I wanna see what type of hoes y'all be fuckin' on behind my back."

"Let's ride then."

CHAPTER TWENTY-EIGHT

I ain't have shit to say so I just grabbed my key and we left.

I hit the unlock button on the key remote of my new car and Lil Tone said, "Damn homie, this you?"

"Yeah, I copped it a few days ago."

Ms. Kelly got me a brand new black-on-black Cadillac off the lot. I just had to pay her five stacks a month until it was paid off.

"You checkin' that bag then, riding in something like this."

"I'm makin' it a lil bit."

I wanted to make him realize just how bad he messed up, so I added, "We about to move in this big ass four-bedroom house, too."

"Nigga, that's more than making it, you doing it."

As I pulled out the alley, April, turned in her seat and said to Lil Tone, "If you stop playing games you can get back on the team."

"I'm done with that other shit. I'm tryin' to get like y'all, so what's up? Can I get back down with y'all?"

Knowing what was about to go down I was quick to agree, "Hell yeah, homie. I don't got nobody else besides April, but she ain't gon be in the streets, so I need you."

"I swear I'm not going to fuck up this time."

"I know you not."

Because you'll be dead before morning, I thought.

We rode most of the way saying nothing. Lil Tone was the only one talking, speaking to April, telling her how bad he was going to do her but I tuned that out.

I waited until I was down the street from the motel before calling Blacky.

He answered and I spoke. "Shorty, I'm about to pull up now. Be ready and have the door unlocked."

"I'm fuckin' him up as soon as he come through the door."

"That's cool. What's the room number?"

I was pulling in the parking spot as he told me the room number.

After hanging up the phone I turned to Lil Tone. "Nigga, you can hit the pussy, but ain't no head poppin' off. That's for me only."

"What about, Lucky?"

"Shit, you can try, but I doubt she'll go."

"That's who y'all came to fuck with? Y'all niggas bogus."

"Shit, she wasn't getting' none so I had to fill the void," I said. "Then you know it ain't no fun if the homie can't have none."

I gave Lil Tone some dap. "Fuck all this talking tho, let's go do this."

Lil Tone got out the car first and I waited until the door was closed before I said to April, "Shorty, I wish yo ass will stay in the car."

"Hell naw, this got to do with me, too."

"Alright, I'm not about to argue with you right now, but stay behind me until we get in the room and don't touch shit in the room."

She just smiled and got out the car.

All I could do is shake my head as I put on my gloves and took my banga out.

I got out the car but left the key in the ignition. Lil Tone was so focused on getting to the room, that he didn't even realize that I had my gloves on and banga out.

"Man, what room we in, 'cause I'm ready to go."

"27," I said.

He walked off towards the stairs and I was right behind him. I was happy to see nobody was around. I just hope nobody was peeking out the windows.

This nigga practically ran to the room and opened the door. I was expecting Blacky to hit him as soon as he walked through the door so I put my gun in front of me just in case he tried to run.

Lil Tone walked in the room and when he saw that it was empty, he turned and looked at me. He saw the gun in my hand, his eyes grew big.

"What the-"

Blacky came from behind the door, hitting Lil Tone, and putting the nigga to sleep.

"Damn, nigga. What yo ass was in here practicing that shit?"

"That bitch tried to kill me."

He went to where Lil Tone was laying and kicked him in the face.

"Wake yo hoe ass up so you can feel the pain before you die."

He started moaning as he came to it. He looked at me all

confused. I knew it was over with for him but I had to tell him we knew.

"Nigga, it ain't no room in this world for a snitch and a snake. Yo bitch ass could've been living good like us, but you had to pull some hoe shit."

"They was taking my spot."

He tried to sit up but I pointed my gun at him making him lay back down.

"Dude, you sound like a straight bitch right now, and that's how you gon' die, bitch."

"You going to kill me? What about my Moms?"

"I'm not about to kill you but you about to die. As for your ma, she should've had a girl instead of a bitch nigga." I smacked him in the face with the banga, opening his shit up. He held his face as crimson blood leaked through his finger, dripped down his hand and stained the carpet.

I turned to Blacky. "It's on you, homie."

Blacky pulled out his .45 and stood over Lil Tone, and April grabbed him by his shoulder.

"That's going to make too much noise and people going to get nosy."

Seeing April as his last hope, Lil Tone shook his head slowly as he began to plead. "April, please don't let them do this to me."

April screwed her face up and sucked her teeth. "Shut yo bitch ass up! So, how we gonna do it 'cause he ain't leavin' here alive."

"April, don't-"

Blacky cut him off with a kick to the face, bussing his nose and sending him back holding his face. More blood leaked.

"Let me do it," April said.

I knew Blacky was going to say no so I asked him what he thought.

Blacky shrugged. "She got a point about the gun so if she got a better way, she can do it."

I didn't want her to do it but, I didn't want to argue with her. "Do you, shorty, if that's what you wanna do."

"Give me them gloves."

I took my gloves off, handed them to her, and wondered what she was about to do. It didn't take long for us to figure it out because as soon as she got the gloves on, she pulled out a knife I didn't even know she carried.

Lil Tone's eyes grew wide with fear. "April..."

She didn't answer. She looked to me and I could see it in her eyes that she was for real about this shit. I knew that April was down for me and the game I was playing but this was on another level. She turned to Lil Tone and approached him with the blade out.

Lil Tone sat up and stretched his arms out. "April! Come on! Y'all, quit playin'. I said I was sorry!" Seeing that his words were falling on deaf ears he said, "Man, fuck that. Help! Somebo-"

Me and Blacky were on him, attacking him from both sides.

"Hel-" I cut him short with a haymaker right to the mouth. He turned to hop up, but

Blacky caught him in a chokehold. I cocked back and punched him in the stomach as hard as I could and he folded.

"Hold him up, Blacky!"

Blacky yanked him up back, pulled him to the floor, and I was on him. Wrestling him to the floor, we held him down and covered his mouth. He struggled to get free but it was useless. April walked over and stood directly over him. Face void of emotion, she squatted and put the blade across his throat as he continued to struggle. Lil Tone released a muffled scream just before she slit his throat, making blood gush profusely. April jumped back as his blood came squirting out, and in that moment, I knew she was down for whatever.

Lil Tone's eyes were bucking as he choked and suffocated on his own blood. Sweat broke across his forehead, and in his eyes, he knew fear as he realized this was the end. His body twitched and spasmed as the life faded from his eyes and he stared into nothingness. Seconds before he took his last breath. We all sat and looked at the lifeless body of our once homie and family, a pool of blood below his neck and head area staining the cream-colored carpet.

April was the first one to speak. "He betrayed us and paid for it with his life. Now, we can get back to doing what we do."

With nothing else to be said we nodded our heads in agreement and left the room. I wiped the door handle off, just in case any prints were on it.

At the car, I turned to Blacky and gave him a brotherly hug. "Good to still have you with us."

I knew we had just proved to him that he was part of the family. I thought about Lil Tone, who I had once called my bother, and hoped that this was enough for Blacky to be down for us until the end.

———

"Did y'all move in the house, yet?" Mama Kelly asked when she opened the door and saw me standing there.

Three days had passed since the night we murdered Lil Tone. They say the first forty-eight hours of a murder investigation are critical. I gave it an extra twenty-four. Besides moving into my new spot, this was my first time being out and about.

"We slept there for the first-time last night but it's still a few things that we got to do before we really get comfortable."

"Where my babies at?"

"April was tired so she stayed in bed, plus I wanted to holla at you by myself."

"Well, excuse my manners. Come in and have a seat."

I took my shoes off and went to sit down.

I waited until she settled herself in her seat before I said, "They found my homie dead the other night in a motel."

A smile spread across her face.

"Ahh, baby, I'm sorry to hear that. I know he was like a brother to you."

"Yeah, but you know how it is in the streets."

PART THREE

CHAPTER TWENTY-NINE

Bishop and April

APRIL

Dang, where this boy at? He needs to hurry up before I mess the whole living room up and have this baby right here. I grabbed my phone and was just about to call him again but I heard him at the door.

"April! April! Where you at?"

"Boy, quit all that yelling. I'm in the living room."

He came back to where I was at.

"What the hell took you so long? You was supposed to be here ten minutes ago."

"Girl, stop playing. I was thirty minutes away. I broke every law possible to get here, you only called ten minutes ago."

"Well, hurry up and help me to the car before we don't gotta go to the hospital."

That got him moving and I don't know how, but he pretty much carried my big ass to the car. He put me in and I settled in my seat while he ran back to get the baby's clothes. We bought stuff for a boy and a girl since we didn't want to know and it didn't go unnoticed that he came out with the girl's bag first. Everything in the car at last, he got in.

"Mama Kelly gon' meet us at the hospital."

He put the key in the ignition, cranked up the car, and pulled off. "I know. I called her until she wouldn't pick up the phone no more."

I started laughing but stopped when I started having contractions. "Boy, you better drive faster."

"I'm trying to make it in one piece, just sit back, shorty."

I wanted so bad to argue, but it was pointless. So, I just sat back and tried to control my breathing. I caught Bishop steady looking over at me.

"Why you keep looking at me like that?"

"Because yo ass better not fuck up my car. I just finished paying for it."

"Make me laugh if you want to. We going to see how good yo ass was paying attention in those classes."

"Yeah, we'll see, but it'll be on the sidewalk."

"Boy, I'm fucking you up when this over."

"Yeah, I love you too."

"I know, baby."

Since I started showing he has waited on me like I was a queen and he dealt with all my mood swings. Truth be told, I had to repay him big time. I waited until he was down the street before I told him who else was going to be at the hospital.

"I called Amanda and she said she wanted to be here, just in case we need her."

I didn't know how he was going to take that so it made my day when he smiled and grabbed my hand. No words were needed as we sped the rest of the way there. We reached West Suburban Hospital in record time.

"This lady is crazy. Look at her."

I looked up and saw Mama Kelly with our doctor and about ten nurses at the emergency room entrance. She saw the car she started waving us over. Before Bishop could even stop the car, she had my door open.

"Come on, baby. Let's go get my grandbaby out of you."

I could see it in all the nurse's faces that she had them moving at the snap of her fingers and just as I had the thought, she snapped her fingers and the nurse with the wheelchair came up.

I started laughing, even though it hurt like hell as I sat in the chair.

"Mama, I hope you been nice to these people."

"Girl, they just doing their jobs and it's going to be the best when it comes to you. Now, can some of y'all help my son with the bags?"

I tuned her out when the doctor came up to me.

"How long has it been since your water broke?"

"Like thirty minutes."

"And how far apart are the contractions?"

"The last one was about a minute ago and..."

Just as I was saying it, I had another one.

"Well, you're a little early but it should be okay, so let's get you upstairs."

I looked around for the first time and saw Amanda. She smiled at me, letting me know she was there. Bishop came running through the door just as we got to the elevator. He stood beside me and held my hand as we rode up.

When we got to the delivery room one of the nurses stopped and turned to us. "Only the father from this point."

Mama Kelly wasn't trying to hear that. "Lady, move on out the way."

"Ma'am, it's hospital rules."

"That's my family and if they don't come in, I'm not having this baby."

I was just talking because it felt like this baby was ready to jump out but I hope they wouldn't argue with me.

"Everybody can come in but you two ladies have to stand off to the side."

I started getting weak and tried to relax as I laid on the bed. They put my legs up and moved my gown out the way. I felt exposed as everybody started taking turns looking at me. I didn't care, as long as they got this over with.

"Okay April, it's ready to come out. I'm going to give you a shot for pain, but I still need you to do as we practiced, okay?"

I nodded my head. Bishop stood on my side, dressed in scrubs and grabbed my hand.

"Baby, it's gon' be alright."

He bent down and kissed me and after that everything was a blur. All I remember was pushing and then the sound of crying.

Before I fell asleep Bishop whispered, "She's beautiful. Thank you."

BISHOP

It seemed like as soon as they let me hold her, they took her right back, so I was stuck at this window, looking at her. She was so tiny but they said that everything was good with her. All she needed was to gain weight. I could tell which baby was mine without it, but it made me smile to see Jasmine Aliza Thompson, August 16, 1999, on her name tag. The life I had planned for her, I had no room for mistakes. Just the short time that I held her and just sat there watching her, I couldn't understand how any man could walk out on their kids.

I felt a hand on my shoulder and looked up to see Mama Kelly and Amanda.

I addressed Amanda first. "Thanks for coming."

"I couldn't have missed it if I wanted to. I just know it's going to be twice as hard for me with these twins."

When we found out that she was having twins we all wanted to know what she was having. We were told, they were a boy and girl, and she didn't waste any time telling me their names were to be John and Janelle. The only thing that I didn't like was they wasn't going to have my last name. She told me that if it was found out that I was the father of her kids that she'll go to prison and the kids would be put in the system. I understood and respected it, but I didn't like it.

"You know we going to be there for you the same way?"

"You better be."

We got quiet for a while before she asked, "Why did y'all change her middle name?"

"That's the way she wanted it and it ain't no way to win no argument with a pregnant woman."

"She's so pretty. Look just like you."

"Ain't she?"

The only thing I saw of April in her was her eyes.

"Well, since everything is good, here. I guess I'll go, now. I still got work to do."

"Alright, I'll call you later, tonight."

She left, leaving me and Mama Kelly alone, watching Jasmine sleep.

"You know you crazy, right?"

"Why would you say something like that?"

You would've thought that she was serious but she wasn't able to keep the smile off her face.

"Mama, you had them people scared to do anything without your approval. I just feel sorry for whoever was around when you had Corn."

"Sometimes you got to be a little tough to get things the right way, but Amanda ain't the only one with work to do."

I know she was talking about me but I didn't plan on leaving yet.

"I didn't know that you had a job now. Where you work at?"

She tried hitting me in the head but I moved.

"Boy, I'm talking about you. The block don't stop for nobody and you need to go get your money."

"The block good. Blacky out there handling the business. Plus, April will kill me if I leave before she wakes up. I'm good here."

"She knows what's up and all that matters is that you was here for the main part. I will be here and when she wakes up, I'll have her call you, okay?"

I smiled. "Do I got a choice?"

"If you go, yeah, but if you try to stay then I'll just kick you out."

"I guess I'll go handle the business but when I'm done, I'm coming right back."

She waved me off, I blew my daughter a kiss and left.

I didn't waste no time calling Blacky and telling him the news. He told me that he and Lucky will be by the hospital later.

I told him I was on my way to the block now. I didn't go straight to the block, though. I rode around, thinking how everything fell into place after we got Lil Tone out the way four months ago. Everything was running as planned and once everybody found out that we were back down, all of our old workers came back and brought friends, too. Hell, on top of that, I finally got enough hangtime to get my hair braided so I did.

The only thing that bothered me about killing Lil Tone was going to see his mom after. When she opened the door, just one look told me that she just got done crying. She tried to act like she wasn't but her eyes were red and her eyelashes was wet. I brought some weed for her but as I sat and talked to her, I ended up hitting it too.

We got high and talked about the good times but she kept saying, "They tell me that it probably was a female that killed him, fuckin' bitch."

I didn't know what to say to that, being I knew and every time she mentioned or asked how I just shook my head. At one point she started crying so hard that I went to sit next to her to hold her and the next thing I knew she was rubbing on my dick. I tried to stop her but she went down my pants and stroked me until I was hard.

"This ain't right," I said, knowing it was true but I didn't try to stop her as she undid my pants and pulled me out.

Before she took me in her mouth she said, "Please, I need this."

I wasn't going to stop her, but at the same time, I wasn't going to do nothing but sit there. I had my eyes closed, trying to finish quick but she got up and started undressing. When she straddled me, I handed her a condom. I let her ride me until we were both drained. We sat there on the couch with me still inside her. She rolled off me and I took off the condom and turned to her.

"That won't happen again. You Lil Tone's Moms and I wouldn't have done it if he was still living so I'm not going to do it now."

I felt that's what I should've said and I didn't want her to think I took advantage of her while she was weak.

"I know baby, but thank you. I needed that."

I got up and went to the bathroom to clean up. When I got back to the living room, I thought she was sleeping so I took the money I had for her and sat it on the table.

I was getting ready to walk out when she said, "The weed is good, but I need something stronger, I need something to take this feeling away."

"I don't got nothing else. You straight with the weed and some Ol' E."

"It's okay if you don't want to give it to me, but I'll get what I'm looking for one way or the other."

I started to tell her that I'll bring her some but I figured that maybe after she cleared her mind, she'll forget all about it but it didn't happen.

About a month after that I was riding through one of my six spots when I saw one of the workers getting some head in the gangway. I really didn't care that they tricked off but I told them not to do it in the open. I parked and jumped out. I walked up, saw it was Mama T on her knees, and forgot all about homie breaking the rule.

"What the fuck is you doing?"

They both looked up and froze.

I walked up and grabbed her. "Get the fuck up!"

Homie saw that he was in the clear and got out the way.

Mama T looked at me and smiled. "I told you that I'll get it one way or the other, didn't I?"

"So, now you lost all self-respect, huh?"

"Naw, I lost the only thing that I had to live for... my son." Tears welled up in her eyes and threatened to spill over.

I looked her over and realized how much weight she lost but the look in her eyes told me everything. It was a look that I've become all too familiar with.

I didn't regret what was done because it had to be done but she didn't have nothing to do with what her son did. She had always been there for me, so I wasn't about to turn my back on her now.

"What about me? You like my mama, too."

"Not after what we did."

"Tell me this, is there a way for me to get you back on yo shit and off the drugs?"

"This what I'm going to do 'til I can be with my son again."

I felt her pain, but she ain't got to be out here selling her body to get high.

"Come on."

I went over to the nigga that was getting head from her.

"How many bags you got on you?"

"I'm on a fresh pack. What's up?"

"How much money you got?"

"Like seventy-five dollars."

"Okay, give me all that and consider that the ass beating you supposed to be getting."

Homie looked like he wanted to get crazy, but must've thought of Bull and handed the money over. When I got back on, one of the lil homies introduced me to this nigga named Bull, a five-foot-five, brown skin stocky guy with a baby face that made him not look like the killer he is. He rocks a fade and on his right side is a facial burn along his jawline. He had a name in the streets for being a shooter and told me that he would be my enforcer if I bought him and his guy's guns. All he wanted was seven-thousand-five-hundred dollars a month.

I handed it all to Mama T. "Make this shit last and start eating. My number the same, use it. Now, move around."

I waited until she was gone before I addressed homie again.

"If she come around again, call me. Don't do that shit with her no more and use the car next time. That's one of the reasons why it's out here."

"Alright, Big Homie. My bad."

I was pulled back to reality by my phone ringing.

I picked up. "What's good?"

"Man, how many times you going to circle the block?"

"I was just thinking about some shit."

"Well, pull over so we can pop this bottle real quick."

Normally, I don't drink but I had a cup of Moet to celebrate with Blacky.

CHAPTER THIRTY

April

"Baby, why you look so mad? You been mugged up for the last week." I had been watching Bishop as I breastfed Jasmine.

"Shorty, it seem like niggas want to keep trying me like I'm too nice or something."

I never wanted to be the one to tell him that he was being too nice, but since it was pulling him down at home, I had to say something now.

"Bull is on our team for a reason, so start using him."

"I use him all the time."

"What? For the niggas on the block? They on our team. They might mess up from time to time but our focus should be on the niggas that want to take our place because it's a lot of niggas out there that envy you and will be quick to take you out, so they can be that nigga."

"Baby, I'm not 'that nigga.' I'm just trying to feed my family and make sure we good."

"I don't know how you don't see it, but it ain't too many sixteen-year-olds that got a block, let alone, six of 'em. Then, you got at least ten niggas that cop twenty plus pounds of weed each week.

"You got three kids under six months but they got everything they want and need for years to come, so if you just was trying to feed our family, then we can quit and just do what I've been doing. Open yo eyes, baby, on the street level, you that nigga."

"So, what should I do?"

That's one thing that I liked about Bishop. He wasn't scared to ask my opinion and when I gave it, he'd use it.

"If niggas sense weakness, they'll play on it. It ain't no room for disrespect in this game, so the next nigga you feel try you, send Bull and his people to go holla at them."

I saw that he was thinking it over, so I focused my attention on breastfeeding Jasmine.

She was so cute looking just like her daddy. I was scared at first, thinking I would have time to do nothing else, but she was quiet and always seemed to know when I was busy.

"So, how much you make to cook up?" Bishop asked me.

"Off a key, I'll make twenty-five-hundred."

"That's decent, especially since you got a good clientele going on."

"Yeah, it's cool, but I give it all to Mama Kelly to put up for your kids so they ain't got to depend on the streets when they get older."

"That what's up, but check it, I got a few hours so when you going to get down again so I can watch and try to learn?"

"When she gets finished, she'll be ready for a nap, so we can do it, then."

Not even fifteen minutes later, I laid Jasmine down in her crib and turned on the baby monitor, just in case she woke up.

I told Bishop everything that I needed so when I got to the kitchen everything was ready. I wasn't used to having somebody there with me and I never taught nobody.

I got the half of key of our shit.

"Okay, this how I do it..."

I went on to put the powder cocaine and baking soda in jars, making sure that everything was even. I then took out the bottle of Remy.

"What's that for?"

"This my mom's favorite drink, so instead of using water, she used Remy. It was her way to put her name on it and it got a different taste to it, so the customers knew who shit they smoking."

"You use that with all the shit you cook up?"

"Naw, I use gin with their shit."

He didn't ask no more questions, so I went on and explained what I was doing.

"I add a little at a time 'til it's like pancake batter and stir it to make sure it ain't no air bubbles."

He listened and watched everything I did. I took the jars out the pot and got the finished product out so he could see how it was supposed to be, then I let him do it.

He finished and I looked it over. I nodded. "You had a good teacher."

———

"Amanda, what's up?"

"Oh nothing, just trying to keep up with these babies. They're growing so fast."

Me and her got real cool since we had our babies. She took a couple of months off work and we spent most of the days together. She started working again and would drop the twins off over here. This was a first for both of us and we were learning together, with the help of Mama Kelly, of course.

"Girl, I need your help setting something special up," I told Amanda,

"I'll help if I can. What is it?"

"You know that since I've known Bishop that he never celebrated his birthday and I wanted to put something together for him."

"He ain't going to want nothing big. You know how he is about stuff like that."

"I was thinking around twenty people or so. Just family and a few close friends."

I were going to plan a special night for us but a few days ago I got a call from Hectic and he put it in my head to have a get together.

Me and Amanda spent the next fifteen minutes going over what we were going to do before she had to go to work. She left and I called everybody I knew Bishop would approve of and told them. Later that night when Amanda came to pick up the twins, she told me that she had the back room reserved at a restaurant downtown.

———

BISHOP

"April, I don't get why you ain't have Mama Kelly watch the kids. I don't know that girl like that."

"Baby trust me, she good so don't worry yourself about that. Let's just enjoy the night."

I wasn't trying to stress over it but this was the first time we left the kids alone with anybody outside of the family. I looked at my braids and saw how good she did them.

"Damn, shorty, why you don't do my shit like this all the time?"

"Because tonight yo special night."

"Yeah, but if my shit don't be fresh like this all the time, I'm gonna cut this shit."

"Stop playing with me and get dressed so we can go."

As I got dressed in the cream linen fit she picked out for me. I thought about my mama wishing she was here with me so I could show her the good life but I pushed those thoughts out my mind, then went and gave my future kisses before we left the crib. I didn't' know where we were going, so I let April drive.

We got downtown and she parked in front of Prime and Provisions on LaSalle Street, where two dudes came and opened our doors. Inside, April gave them our name and after finding it, a waitress came and we followed her through the restaurant to the back.

Before she opened the door, April, grabbed my hand. "Don't be mad at me."

The door opened and I saw Hectic, Blacky and Lucky, Mama Kelly, Bull and a few niggas from his crew, the Twins, Amanda, some of the faithful workers I trusted and some of the niggas that was spending big on the weed. I was surprised but I loosened up and went in smiling.

"If y'all asses would've jumped out on me, I swear I would've left."

The doors closed and everybody began kicking it. I made my way around the room to holla at everybody that came. I was trying to make my way over to Hectic but every time I stopped, then looked up again, he'll be on the other side of the room. I knew he was trying to avoid me because he wasn't talking to nobody and therefore had no reason to move. I knew if I messed up, he would've told me about it.

Finally, after an hour, I was done talking to everybody and it was time to eat. April came to me with a plate already made and led me to where Hectic was already sitting, then left us alone.

"Happy birthday, young hustla."

"Good lookin', homie."

I learned that sometimes it's best to let Hectic take his time to get to what's on his mind. I could tell this was one of the times.

"I hate crowds, especially with a bunch of people I don't know. I wish I wouldn't have had April do this."

"That's what you get, but I hate crowds, too, even if I know 'em."

"Yeah, we got a lot of the same likes and dislikes. That's why I mess with you."

"Don't lie, you mess with me 'cause I make you good money."

It's not too often that you'll hear him laugh but when he did you know it's sincere. You'll even see his young age.

"That's a plus but I see myself in you and I know like me you don't fuck with that flashy shit but I had to get this for you."

He put a jewelry box on the table and pushed it to me. I grabbed it and looked inside. It was a gold chain and the Bishop chess piece with crushed diamonds around it.

"I saw it and had to get it for you. That's solid gold and real diamonds but I knew you'll like it because I like it."

"Yeah, I like it. This something I can wear." I put it on. "Good lookin', homie. I appreciate it."

"Man, that ain't all I got for you, though. It's some people that I want you to meet. Really, they want to meet you."

This was the reason for all the small talk.

"Alright, but what it's all about?"

"They want to meet the biggest moneymaker that any of us got, especially when I told them your age."

"That's cool. When we gonna do that?"

"I'll let you know, but it'll be soon."

He took a sip of water, then stood up.

"I got to go, now. I hope you don't mind, but this ain't my type of party."

"It's all good. Thanks for coming through."

We shook hands and he left. I looked around for April when she popped up with a camera.

"Smile for Corn, baby."

She snapped a picture, then came and hugged me. "We got to make sure Corn feels like he here with us."

"Yeah, that's what's up. We can send a few flicks to yo people, too."

"Why Hectic leave so soon?"

"You know how his kind is. He don't wanna be around all these people."

"And this was his idea, but forget that, you ready to open all your gifts?"

"Not really, but let's do it so we can go."

It was cool for a little bit, but now it really wasn't nothing to do now, so I was ready to go get some birthday pussy. I was used to birthdays with just me and my mama anyways and I didn't want a nigga getting comfortable thinking this was going to be an every year thing.

Most of the niggas gave me money, which I'll just put in the kids' savings but then I got a Pelle, a sound system and a TV for the car from Blacky and Lucky. Mama Kelly gave me gifts cards to a bunch of stores.

One of the boxes I got had twin nines. I had my bitch already, so I tossed them to Bull. "I guess it's your birthday, too, my nigga."

After the gifts, the cake and a little more drinking, April stood up and got the room's attention.

"This party right here is over but it's an after party at the Holiday Inn and it's going to be a lot more people there, especially females, so I hope y'all enjoy y'all selves and the rest of the night! Right now, I got to go give my baby his gifts, so thank y'all for coming."

We stayed at the door and thanked everybody for coming until it was just the family. The restaurant staff helped carry my stuff out to the car and we just stood around kicking it for a few minutes.

"I know that all the ladies had something to do with this, but Blacky, if I found out you was with it, I won't forgive you."

"Man, I swear, I just found out today at the last minute and I tried to call you to give you a 'heads up' but I was followed by somebody."

He cut his eyes at Lucky and everybody started laughing.

"Well, just be happy that lady Lucky was watching over you because I would've got you if you would've fucked all my planning up."

Like a choir, Mama Kelly, the Twins, Amanda and Lucky all said "Yeah" at the same time.

"I would've had yo back but I'll catch up with you in the a.m."

"He must don't know what I'm going to do to his ass. He might holla at you in the a.m. but don't think it's going to be tomorrow's a.m."

Needless to say, she was right. We spent the longest time away from Jasmine since she was born. For the next two days we did nothing but make love, fuck and eat. If it wasn't for April being on birth control now, we would've made more babies.

————

It's been two weeks since the party and shit was going good. As I finished packing my bag for Mexico, I laid down trying to get my nerves under control.

It was a few days before Hectic called me to tell me what's up.

"They're ready to meet with you."

"Alright, I'm ready. You want me to come over there?"

"No, they want you and your girl to fly down to Mexico for a couple of weeks. I will make sure that everything is taken care of, so y'all don't have to go through the normal channel."

"So, when do we leave?"

"Give it like ten to fifteen days. I'll let you know for sure when everything is set up."

I think I was more nervous about flying than meeting with the top people. I never been out of Illinois, let alone another country.

"Baby, get up and help me take these bags downstairs," April said. "The limo should be here soon."

"You packing like we moving down there or something."

"Well, you never know what might happen and I got to be ready for whatever."

"Yeah, whatever, shorty."

The doorbell rang just as I got up and April ran to get it.

"Baby, the ride here. Hurry up."

I took all the bags down to the front door, leaving the driver to take them out.

Mama Kelly came to pick Jasmine up the night before so the only thing I had left to do was make sure the house was locked up.

I thought we were going to one of the big airports but we drove to a city called Joliet. There was this nice ass jet that we pulled up which shocked me, especially when we got inside and it was only us on it. On the ride here I drank some of the liquor that was in the limo's bar, hoping it'll calm me down or at least put me to sleep for the trip.

"Baby, I could get used to this, right here," April said as we looked around.

"Yeah, this shit nice as hell and they got a bed back there."

"You nasty, boy."

"See, I wasn't even talking about that, but that is a good idea."

I gave her that look that I knew she wasn't going to turn down.

The take-off wasn't as bad as I thought it would be and after a few minutes of being in the air, I was able to relax. Not long after the jet ascended, the flight attendant came to ask us if we wanted drinks, then let us know that our meal will be ready in about an hour but if we needed anything before then, simply call.

We had an hour to waste so what better way to spend it than to fuck. I tried to go slow at first but with April moaning and throwing the pussy back at me I started beating it up. Not even five minutes after we were done the flight attendant came in with the food. The look on her face told me she heard all the noise April made.

I didn't eat much before the flight because I was nervous but that was over and I banged everything they put in front of me. I was so full that the only thing I could do was go lay down and get some rest.

I don't know how long I slept, but before long, we were landing in Mexico.

CHAPTER THIRTY-ONE

I really didn't know what to expect as we got off the plane. In movies, I saw it was always some shit about passports but I should've known better than to think I was going to have to go through that. Just as we got dropped off, that's how we were getting picked up, in a limo.

When we were getting ready to pull off, the phone rang. I answered. "Hello."

A voice I didn't know responded, "Is this Bishop?"

"Yeah, this me."

"Okay. You will be dropped off at a hotel. When you get there, give them the name, Michael Frey. When you get to your room it'll be a passport for both you and April. You are to have them on you at all times. There will also be a cell phone for you which I will call you on, so you better not ever part ways with that phone because if you miss my call, you miss your chance."

"When should I be expecting to hear from you?"

"I don't know. It could be in the next hour or the next

month. Just be waiting but in the meantime, it is spring break so it's a lot of stuff going on. Enjoy your trip."

Without another word, he hung up.

I told April what was said. "See why I packed so much? I'd rather be over-prepared than not prepared at all."

"Okay, you told me so, but now what do you want to do while we here?"

"Everything that we can do. I'm ready to have some fun."

Hectic told me a little about Mexico and that's what we spent the ride to the hotel talking about. I told her how she got to go to the tattoo shops to buy weed and other drugs she got excited.

"Baby, can we please get some tattoos? I want some so bad."

"Alright, we can do that. I know a few that I want."

We got to the hotel and everything went just as I was told. Thankfully, it didn't take April half as long to unpack as it did to pack. That handled, we spent time in our room Jacuzzi. April said since she didn't sleep on the plane, she was going to call it a night and start fresh in the morning.

Everything I did, I wanted it to be with my girl so I laid down with her, even though I couldn't sleep. Eventually, I dozed off and, in the morning, I woke up to the phone ringing and the sun in my face.

I answered the phone, thinking it was Dude. "Yeah?"

"What the hell you still doing in bed this late?"

I looked at the bedside clock and saw that it was 11:30.

"Man, I guess I was tired but what's good with you, Hectic?"

"Same thing, different day but how about we meet downstairs in thirty minutes and have a late breakfast?"

I didn't even know he was down here.

"What young hustler, you thought I was going to send you

here by yourself on the first trip? Naw, I had to be here just as much as you did."

"Alright, then let me get up so we can be down there on time."

———

Spring break came and went without another call from Dude, but I wasn't tripping because we were living it up. I think we did just about all there was to do but getting our tattoos was the best part of the trip. We got each other's names on our necks and we both got 'Jasmine' on our wrists. I got my mama's face with her name, birthday, and the day she died on my forearm. April was missing our baby so much, that she'll call Mama Kelly three or four times a day.

We were in a strip club and for the first time in a few days, it seemed like April was having fun again. Sitting back and watching her getting a lap dance had me ready to fuck her right there, but the phone rang. For a second, I didn't know it was mine until I felt it vibrating. I knew it was Dude, just because we were having fun and it seemed that'll be the time he'll call.

I wanted to go where it was quiet but I thought about what he said about me missing his call, so I picked up.

"Hello."

"Be back at your hotel in ten minutes. It'll be a limo waiting on you when you get there."

"Alright. I'll be there."

"And bring April with you."

Just as before, he just hung up.

April was looking at me as I hung up. I motioned for her to come on as I got up. She handed the rest of the money she had to the stripper before she followed me out. By the time she caught up to me a taxi was pulling up to the curb.

She got in, turning to me, "That shit was hot. They just had to call now."

"Yeah, I wanted to crack that right then. I wish we had some time to go to the room."

"How long we got? We might can pull it off."

"I wish. It's gon' take damn near ten minutes to get back and that's all the time he gave us."

She looked at me, confused. "Us?"

"He said to bring you with me."

She still looked confused so I said, "Ay, I didn't know until now but I need you just in case I miss something."

"Baby, you know I got your back. I just didn't expect them to want to see me, too."

"Well, it just might be a good thing, 'cause if they trust you to meet them, then you can handle business with them when I can't."

"Yeah, I guess."

I didn't like the way she said that but I didn't have time to comment on it because we were pulling into the hotel. I paid the cab driver and got out. I looked at the time to see that we just made it. The same driver that picked us up from the airport was there, waiting on us. He opened the back door as we walked up and when I got in, I saw Hectic was there with five other Mexicans. We were seated, and Hectic spoke first.

"Young hustler, what's up?" He then turned to April. "We meet again, Miss Lady."

We didn't get a chance to say nothing before one of the other dudes spoke.

"So, this is Bishop and April. Please don't take offense to

this, but I thought I'll be seeing the typical black kid trying to dress like a rap star, especially with all the money I know that you two are making."

The guy sitting next to him nodded his head in agreement.

"None taken. I had good teachers that told me that's a good way to bring heat and get popped off."

"Yes, I liked Mr. Corn's style. Just a shame how he went down."

I was shocked that he knew about Corn but I didn't let it show.

"Yeah, but he'll be good. He ain't the only one, though. Hectic put me up on game, too."

I was wondering who the other guys were but I know it wasn't good to ask questions, so I waited. We rode out the area that was for the tourist into what seemed to be the hood.

After a few minutes of riding in silence, the same guy said, "All this area belongs to me and my brother."

He nodded his head to the guy sitting next to him. "The tattoo shop you went to is ours. We own ten more around here and that's how we sell weed to the college kids. That way we don't do it in the streets to where the police see it like y'all do it in the US."

"But the police still know it goes on, don't they?"

For the first time, his brother spoke. "That's beside the point. Most will overlook what they can't see, even if they know what's going on. I've watched how you run your operation."

He went on to tell me about every spot I had, weed, rocks and even surprised me by knowing about the new blow joint I just opened up.

When I didn't say nothing, he went on to say, "Don't look at it as if your team was slipping because it's my business to know these things and seeing your layout for myself is why we are having this meeting and why we are offering you a special offer."

I expected him to say what it was but when he didn't so I asked, "Which is?"

"We like to make money. That's going to come to me and my brother no matter who we deal with, but we don't want to have to deal with new people every year so we look for people we see have a good head on their shoulders and can stay in the game for a long time."

"We see that in you." That came from the first brother. "But the question is, do you see it?"

I wanted to think about the question before I said something but April started talking first.

"My parents had a fifteen-year run as the King and Queen of Chicago's drug game before they got popped by the Feds and the only thing that both of them said that they regretted was not getting out sooner because they had enough money put up for me to have a good life until I died. With that said, about ten years is a good run."

They looked at each other before the second one said, "I don't know how we missed that. We know of your parents and wished they had worked with us, but this was never so. They had ties to another family. Nevertheless, if you and Bishop become anything like them, we will work out good."

"So, what is this offer you talkin' about?" I looked at the first one, being that he said it.

"First, so we can be on equal grounds as business partners, my name is Jose and this brother of mine is Jesus. Most people know us as the Perez brothers."

Just as he said that his eyes went to the window. I looked and saw a jeep with dudes holding guns. For the first time, the other three guys did something besides sitting there. Out of nowhere, they had choppers in hand, confirming my thought that they were bodyguards.

Jose spoke as if this was a daily thing. "They are harmless. We're in their hood, as you'll probably say in the U.S. and they want to make sure we don't make no stops while here."

He picked up the phone and told the driver to make his way back to the hotel.

Without another glance, he said, "We are offering you unlimited weed for one-hundred-and fifty-thousand per year. And not just any weed. Hydro, or Dro, as your people like to call it. Very few people in your city have this. I know these to be facts. The few that do won't be able to get it in large quantities like you. Subsequently, you will control the market."

"That's the little money, but we offer it to sweeten the pot. Our main offering is cocaine. We will be having a hundred kilos coming your way every two weeks and we need somebody, preferably you, to oversee the distribution of it. What do you think of that?"

"I'm still listening."

It all seemed too good to be true, and in most cases, it is. I was hoping that this wasn't one of the times.

"Okay, I guess you want to know about the money. Well, we sell a kilo for thirteen. You keep three from each you move, and you pay eight for the ones you buy yourself. You don't have to worry about contacting anybody, they will get at you. All you have to do is watch over the shipment when it gets there and collect the money. Our people will do the drop-off when you give them the go.

I was thinking about everything he said before I realized we were back at the hotel.

"Can you give us some time to think it over before we give you an answer?"

"Of course, but you only have until tomorrow, your plane leaves at ten. I will ride to the airport with you to get your answer and if there's something more that you think you should get, I'll be happy to listen."

"Okay, we'll be ready by then."

The driver opened the door and I shook their hands but Jesus held on before saying, "I like how y'all handled that situation that put Corn where he is. That's what happens to rats."

I nodded, letting him know I got the message. After shaking Hectic's hand, me and April got out.

Back in our room, I ordered room service and April went to shower. The food made it just as she finished. We talked as we ate and came up with what we wanted to do.

The next day Jose pulled up to the plane and I told him we were cool with the offer. It ain't no way to turn that down or try to ask for more but we cut the time down to five years.

He smiled before saying, "Smart move. Real smart move. I will set it up and Hectic will give all the details you need." We shook hands but this time to seal our deal.

CHAPTER THIRTY-TWO

3 Years Later

"Yo, what's up?" I was on my way to have my monthly meeting with Hectic at a low-key steak house downtown called, The South Loop Club off State Street. I was by Robert Morris when the phone rang.

"Man B, where you at?"

It was Bull and the tone of his voice told me something was wrong.

"Man, I'm out and about. What's good?"

"We got to talk, but not on the phone."

"Alright, where you at now?"

I didn't think that he'd try to set me up but for the three years since I've been on the team with Jose and Jesus and been getting more of the game from Hectic, I've learned to assume nothing and question everything.

"I'm at the crib on 16th and St. Louis."

"Just meet me on West End in the school parking lot."

"I'll be there."

We hung up.

I thought of going to tell Hectic face to face that something came up but I settled for calling him, just in case it was something that couldn't wait. He picked up on the first ring and I told him what I knew.

"He didn't give you a hint?"

"Naw, but he never called over no little shit before so I didn't want to ask him nothing over the phone."

"I feel you but send somebody through there first to make sure he by himself and ain't nobody trying to lure you in no trap."

"Yeah, I'll do that."

"Well, call me when you know something and we'll have to wait until sometime next week before we can meet again because I'm going out of town but I'll let you know exactly when we can meet up as soon as I get back."

"Alright, I'll get up with you later on this situation, whatever it is."

We hung up and I called Blacky.

"Homie, I need you to have somebody go sit on the West End and watch Austin parking lot to make sure Bull come by himself."

"I'm down the street on the block. You want me to do it?"

"Yeah, that's straight, but try not to be seen and call me back in like twenty minutes and tell me what it look like."

"I got you homie but is it anything I need to know?"

"Shit. I don't know what's going on but I need you to be my eyes for now."

"I'm on my way, right now. One."

"One."

I tried to think of everything that could've went wrong but

everything I thought of didn't seem possible. I was coming up with nothing. It only took me fifteen minutes to get back to the hood so I called Blacky to see if it was straight to come through. He said Bull just got there and he wasn't with nobody. I told him to keep his eyes open and then, I called Bull.

"I'm about to pull up. Come, get in my car."

"I'll be on the corner then."

I turned down Pine, made a right at the West End and picked him up. I saw Blacky's car on Lotus facing towards the right. It was a one way but I still turned down his way so he knew to follow me. With him behind me, I focused my attention on Bull.

"Man, what's up now?"

"I fucked up, homie."

"How's that?"

I knew Bull was a gangsta, and a good nigga to have on my side instead of against me, but right now he seemed like a kid and it was new to me.

"Two of the cribs got hit in Holy City."

"What?!"

I wasn't really mad at him but hearing them words made my blood boil. "Was it the police or some niggas?"

"It was some niggas."

"So, how the fuck did it happen?"

I was mad as hell but I knew I had to put my emotions to the side so I could think clear.

"I got a call from the homie at the Lawndale spot. When I was getting the story from over there, I got a call from the Hamlin spot with the same shit."

"So, how much did they get us for?"

"I'm not sure of the exact amount but it's in the twenty thousand range. They didn't get to the backroom in the Lawndale spot and that's where most of the day's earnings at."

"Twenty stacks. That's real fucked up, but where you fuck up at?"

"I let some bitch ass nigga rob you, that's how I fucked up!"

Even though I didn't think I could in this situation, I started laughing.

"Homie, you a good nigga, but you ain't superman. You didn't know that shit was gon' happen. That's a big loss, but surprisingly, this the first time it happened in over three years. Now, we just gotta put more guns and better S at the spots."

"Yeah, I agree that we got to step the security up, but I'm not accepting that loss."

"Don't stress yourself over that shit, homie. The streets will talk and when we find out who was involved, it'll get handled."

"That's not the point. I know who did it and I should know where they'll be tonight in about an hour."

"Shit, in that case, handle yo business. Find out where they gon' be, get yo team together and meet me back over here, in an hour."

"What, you riding with us?"

"Fuck you mean am I riding with y'all? Them niggas robbed me. I'm not gon' sit back after no shit like that."

"I feel you, homie."

I dropped him back off at his car before I called Hectic and told him what happened. I let him know it would be taken care of before the night was over. Blacky pulled up and parked beside me. He heard everything so I didn't have to repeat the situation. He wanted to ride with us but I explained to him that he was needed on the block.

I went back home to explain the situation to April and told

her that I was going to go with Bull and get our shit back. I kind
of thought she was going to argue but she told me that we had to
send the message loud and clear that we ain't accepting no shit
like that and if somebody tries again, they'll know we coming for
them.

She drove me back out west. I told her that I'll get a ride
home before I kissed her and Jasmine, who was sleep. Bull had
five of the guys that I heard was knocking niggas shit back for
sport. He was talking to them when I walked up. Seeing me, he
wrapped it up and pulled me to the side.

"Man, homie, it was some niggas from out south that got us.
They on 61st and Carpenter."

"Do I know any of them?"

"Naw, we just got lucky that one of the workers saw one of
the cars after they hit the spot and he said dude used to fuck
with his sister and from there we found out what we know
now."

That didn't make sense. "Wait a minute. There's probably a
million cars of the same model all over America. What makes
you so sure this is-"

"Custom plates," Bull said, cutting me off. "The car has
custom plates."

These guys have to be the most dumbest criminals ever. I
shrugged. "So, what the plan is?"

"First thing first, we gonna get the money back. Then it's
whatever you want to happen but we want to lay whoever in the
house down."

"Alright, say it go down just like that. Is something gon' come
of it?"

He thought about it before he said, "If you talking about a
war, I doubt it but they might have a few niggas that might

come through and take a few pop shots but it ain't shit we can't handle."

"Alright, I trust yo judgment, let's ride."

"You strapped, right?"

I just looked at him and walked to his Jeep. He got in next to me and I pulled the 9mm out and sat it on my lap. He looked and nodded his head, knowing that was a dumb question.

There wasn't much to say on the ride out south, but my mind was racing with thoughts. I tried to block them out to stay focused on the task at hand. I was happy that the ride didn't take long. I was watching the streets and I knew we got off the Dan Ryan on 63rd and not long after that, I heard the two guys in the back seat cocking their guns. Bull called the other car and told them to go through the alley and we'll take the front.

We waited a second before flying down the block. The Jeep hopped the curb and before I knew it, they were out the car and kicking the door open. I got out and caught up with them as they went through the door. As I came in, the back door came flying open and the rest of the team came running in. We caught three niggas sitting on the couch counting my money on the table in the front of them. The drugs were sitting in stacks off to the side like they hadn't been messed with yet. Within reach were two handguns between the drugs and money and a shotgun leaned up against the couch, but when they saw all the guns pointed at them, they threw their hands up.

Bull walked up to one of them and slapped him with the banga. "Nigga, you thought you was gonna get away with this shit? Bitch nigga, ain't shit sweet!"

The guy he hit wiped blood from his face. "You got that fam. You know how this shit go, we get money doin' the stick up shit, but it ain't personal so don't make it. Just take y'all shit back and slide."

He said that shit like it was really going to work. I was about to say something when Bull turned to me. "This the leader of the crew. I got something special for him. Y'all load this shit up so we can finish this and bounce."

I kept my gun aimed at the nigga in front of me as two of the guys stuffed everything back in the duffle bags that were around the table. I was the closest one to the front door and I turned as I heard a noise. I saw the shadow before the first person came through the door. I tried to swing my pistol around but it was too late.

Boom! Boom!

I didn't feel the shots hit me, but my legs felt like rubber as I fell. I squeezed the trigger as I went down. The shots only hit the wall but it was enough to push him back out the door. Shots were going off from everywhere. My ears were ringing. I could no longer feel my arm and couldn't lift my hand to shoot. So, I laid there.

Just as fast as the shooting started, it stopped. I saw people running out the back door but couldn't tell if it was Bull and his team or the other niggas. I tried to stand up but my legs wouldn't support me. I looked around me and saw that all the niggas that was sitting on the couch was shot up and another one was laid out by the door. Hearing the sirens in the distance I started dragging myself across the floor to the backdoor. When I finally made it, the sirens were right outside and that's the last thing I remembered before passing out, then waking up in the hospital, handcuffed to the bed.

———

The doctor and nurse finished examining me and signed off for me to be released. They said that I had a gunshot wound to the leg and stomach and a graze wound to my shoulder. I spent the last thirteen hours in the hospital and since I've been awake, it's been a police officer sitting next to my bed.

"Where my clothes at?"

"They were bloody and were thrown in the trash but everything else is in your bag." He lifted a bag from the hospital as he said it.

"Where am I going now?"

"To the 51st and Wentworth police station."

"So, I'm under arrest then?"

"As of now, you are but it all depends on how your interview with the homicide detectives goes."

I knew enough to stay quiet and say nothing that would incriminate me. I just followed their orders after they put the handcuffs on me. Luckily, they were in the front because my shoulder was hurting bad. It wasn't a long ride to the police station and once getting there, they put me in a room with nothing but two chairs, in between which was a four-leg rectangle table. I was offered something to eat but all I wanted was something to drink. I sat there for close to an hour with the feeling that somebody was watching me the whole time then somebody finally came in.

A skinny white detective dressed in slacks, a white dress shirt and a light brown suit coat entered without a word and sat in the other chair, going through some papers in a folder. He looked more like a science nerd to me more than anything, with those big glasses and beady eyes. His hair was a greying brown and it was thinning. It was like that for another five minutes. I was getting ready to ask him what's up but another cop came in. This time it was a female, a pale white brunette with a thin nose wearing khakis and an off-brand white polo shirt. I could tell she ain't have no ass. It was obvious she had an attitude, and I smiled on the inside thinking that was probably why. Either that or she was gonna play the "bad cop," a role in one of the law enforcement's oldest tricks in the book. That would make Poindexter sitting across from me the "good cop." She came in with another chair and didn't waste no time getting down to business.

"Your name, John Thompson. Date of birth, February 19, 1983, right?"

"Yeah."

"Okay, I'm Detective Brandenburg, and this is my partner Detective Harris. Now, before you try to be a dumb ass and say you want a lawyer, let me tell you a few things so we can skip the bullshit and we can help each other and all of us in this room will be sleeping in their own bed, tonight. Do you want to listen?"

I shrugged my shoulders and she said, "Okay, we have a house with four people dead and two were on the way to the hospital. You were one of them and the other one looks like he'll be victim number five, making you the only person that knows what happened. You following me, right?"

I nod.

"Okay. Now I must read you your rights before I ask you any more questions."

She got a piece of paper from the guy cop who had yet to speak. She then read me my rights, checking each one off as she went.

When she was done, she said, "If you understand your rights, sign at the bottom."

She handed me the paper and pen, I signed it and handed it back. She signed, too, and gave it back to her partner.

"Since you understand your rights, do you want to talk to us and answer a few questions?"

"I guess I gotta talk to tell you I want a lawyer." I started laughing at the dumb look on her face.

Both of them stood up and the guy cop said, "Well, I guess your lawyer will be telling you that you are charged with four first-degree murders with a possible fifth one. Have a nice life, you piece of shit."

CHAPTER THIRTY-THREE

April

"When this boy gets here, I swear I'm fucking him up."

I've been pacing for the last hour, worrying about Bishop. I wasn't tripping too much when he left because it was something he had to do but when I hadn't heard from him in hours, I wasn't able to sleep. Now it's been over twenty-four hours and I had a million things running through my mind and none of them were good.

I grabbed my cell phone off the table and pressed the "send" button and listened as his phone went straight to his voicemail again. I wanted to throw it so bad, but I thought about it and sat it back down.

"Twin, this nigga gonna make me kill him when he come home."

"You never know April, they're probably still handling the business. He good, though."

That did it right there.

I snapped. "No, the fuck he ain't good, bitch! You know Bishop ain't never about to not check-in if not for me, then you better believe he making sure Jasmine is straight. Hectic ain't heard from him, either. You know something real fucked up because Bull not even answering his phone. Twin, I can feel it. Something happened to him... I can feel it."

Twin just looked and I could tell she was thinking the same thing. With those words spoken, I lost all energy and sat on the couch. I don't know how long I sat there before Jasmine came and sat on my lap. I held her and kissed her forehead when the first tear fell.

"I miss Daddy. Mommy, when is he coming home?"

"Hopefully soon, baby, because he knows we missing him and I know he miss us."

"Can we call him, Mommy?"

"Yeah, go get Mommy's phone and bring it here."

Jasmine got off the couch and ran to get my phone. She returned with it in hand, and as soon as she handed it to me, it started ringing. I didn't wait to see who it was before answering.

"Bishop!"

It was a short pause before I got my answer.

"Naw, April, it's me. I was calling to see if you heard anything from him or anybody else, but I see you ain't heard shit."

"Blacky, I don't know what the fuck's going on. I can't get ahold of him or Bull."

"Bull right here with me. He..."

"He with you. Then where is Bishop? They left together. Blacky, tell me what the fuck's going on! What happened to Bishop, Blacky?

I was crying hard because I knew whatever he was going to tell me was going to be bad news.

"Chill out, April. I'm trying to tell you, now."

"I'm listening. What's going on?"

"Look, it's not for sure, but when they were handling the business they got ambushed and Bishop got hit."

I don't know what else he said. My world went black and it felt like I was falling.

I thought it was Jasmine shaking me at first, but then I caught my man's name and looked to see Twin holding the house phone out to me.

"Bishop on the phone, girl. Here, take it."

I snatched it, part of me not believing he was really on the phone after hearing what Blacky said. But part of me wanted to hold onto hope.

"Hello! Baby! Where you at? Please tell me that you okay!"

I held my breath, waiting to hear his voice.

"Baby, I'm good but I need you to stay strong for me. Naw, stay strong for us, alright, Shorty?"

"But they said you..."

I couldn't' finish the sentence. Tears of joy poured from my eyes, knowing that whatever it was from here, I could deal with it.

"Shorty, fuck what they said. Everything's all good. I'm in a little jam but I'm good."

"Where you at?"

"I got arrested. They got me on 51st and Wentworth right now but they probably gon' take me to the County Jail. I need you to call Hectic and let him know I need him to get a good ass lawyer, no matter how much it cost."

"Okay, baby. I'll do that, but what they got you on?"

"Right now, they say it's four bodies but it might be another one."

"Baby, I know you can't talk too much on the phone, but please tell me you didn't give them no statement."

"Shorty, I'll probably be mad any other time for you asking some shit like that, but I don't got a lot of time, so I'll let that shit fly."

"Baby, I'm sorry. Did you get shot?"

"Yeah, it wasn't shit though. Where Jasmine at?"

"She right here."

"Baby, Blacky on the cell, right now."

"Well, let me talk to my baby real quick and you tell Blacky that I need him to step up for me and I'll get at him when I can."

I grabbed the phone from Jasmine and handed the other one to her.

"Daddy wants to talk to you."

I then said to Blacky, "Bishop on the other phone, right now. They got him locked up but he said he'll get at you."

I heard him tell somebody, probably Bull in the background what I just told him before he said, "Let him know we got him with whatever needs to be done. Just let us know."

"Well, I'll call you when I find out everything, but for now, I'm going to need you to do more to keep this shit we got going."

"April, that goes without saying. I'll come by the crib early tomorrow morning."

"I'll see you then."

I hung up with him and Jasmine handed me the house phone back. I let him know everything Blacky said but then they said he had to go. I knew what I had to do but I had to sit back and get myself together before I could go again.

I called Hectic and told him everything Bishop told me.

"Okay, I'll have the lawyer get all the info we need and he'll handle everything on that level but can you handle everything on y'all end."

"Don't worry about that. I'll make sure everything runs the same, just help me get Bishop back home."

He assured me that the lawyer was the best and would do all that could be done. Before we hung up, we agreed to meet next week.

"Twin, I need some sleep. Why don't you take Jasmine out to eat and put her to bed for me?"

Five minutes after they left, I was knocked out.

———

BISHOP

"Ay, homie. They call you Bishop?"

I just got back from a visit with April and I was sitting in my bed reading the letter I got from her yesterday. I looked up and saw three Mexicans standing at my door.

"Yeah, what's up?"

A lot of niggas I came across knew who I was but I didn't really know none of them.

"I just got off the phone with my family and I heard you know my cousin, Hectic."

"Naw, I don't know nobody by that name."

I didn't know who they were, but I know my celly told me to watch out for the Mexicans because they be on some snake shit and I didn't know if they was lying or not and I wasn't in no shape to be fighting.

They started laughing before he said. "He said you'll say that but he told me to tell you about that chain he gave you at yo party where he told you about some people wanting to meet you. You know who I'm talking about now, young hustler?"

I couldn't help but smile a little and relax.

"Yeah, that's my homie. I was just about to write him."

"He told me that you good people and told me to look out for you. You ain't plugged is you?"

"Naw, I don't have time for that gang shit. I just get money."

"Don't worry about that. The Kings got you, homie. If you want, we got a bunk open that you can get."

"Hell yeah. I need to get off this floor."

"Put yo stuff together and come move in."

I didn't have shit yet so it ain't take no time. They gave me a "no bond" because I ran from DCFS and they say I was a flight risk. I wanted to do a speedy trial but my lawyer told me it'll give the state a chance so it was better to wait. So, with me knowing that I was going to be sitting down for a little bit, I started studying to get my GED. All I do is write letters, work out, and eat all day. I was missing the streets and my freedom but since I had to be here, I made the best of it and was living good.

CHAPTER THIRTY-FOUR

April

I walked into the county jail, dreading the search and violation of me as a human being. Sometimes I was subjected to the taunts of male COs, and other times I was the victim of female COs that gave me a hard time. Today, outside of the search, I was spared the usual tactics they used to make people reluctant to visit their loved ones. Not that it would stop me anyways.

Besides, the COs stayed at the desk to the side, right before the visiting wing entrance. Pass that point, they paid you no mind. Hell, they were subject to leave you. There were times that I was there for a long time, a lot longer than I should've been.

I entered Division Eleven's visiting room and paused when I saw Bishop still hadn't come on the floor. I sighed. It sucked that I had to see him behind the glass, but it beat seeing him in a casket any day so I wasn't complaining. I continued.

There were ten booths but the room was never full, only a

few people there at a time, always. The other visitors were already there so I didn't see them. I chose the last one on the end and sucked my teeth in frustration as I looked around me. It ain't make no sense how run down and dirty this place was. The glass was scratched up, and all the screws and screw holes were rusted out.

I sat down, and while I waited, I heard a guy at one of the other booths spazzed on whoever he was visiting. "Nigga, you need to get your priorities in order! We at war in the streets and you want me to chase some random bitch down? I love you, Bro. Yo kids gone be straight, you gone be good, and your lawyer will be paid. I'ma handle that. But if it ain't got nothing to do with them three things, then miss me with it! Find one of them in the way niggas to do that shit."

It got quiet and I wish I could hear what his homie had to say because what dude was saying was real. Was he trying to get home or fuck with a female that clearly went MIA when he got locked up?

All that went out the window and my focus went to Bishop when he sat down in front of me, smiling. He was in his County get-up, a two-piece tan suit that they call BOC.

"Shorty, what's good with you?"

"Hey, baby. I miss you so much. Your daughter asks about you every day."

"Where she at anyways?"

"Oh, I got to go do something when I leave here, so I left her with Mama Kelly."

"Tell her I love her and give her a kiss for me."

"I will. Amanda told me she was going to bring the twins up here, this week. She be writing you?"

"Yeah, she writes a few times a month. I got like five-hundred pictures of the kids. When I called her, she told me she was coming soon so I was expecting her."

"I talked to the lawyer the other day. He told me where the other guy lived but I already knew all that. He told me to make sure nothing happens to him because he might be some help to our case."

"Yeah, I hear that shit but I don't trust the nigga if he tells what happens to them people, then I'm popped."

I knew what he was saying was true but I had a plan and I hope it works.

I didn't want to tell him yet, but I knew he needed to hear something so I said, "Well, he didn't tell the whole story yet so don't stress yourself over that shit and let me take care of that. Do you got enough money on your books?"

"Yeah, I'll be straight for a couple more weeks."

"I see you getting all fat in here. I guess I wasn't feeding you good enough."

"Oh, I see you got jokes but this all muscle and you gon' see when I get out and fold you up."

"What? You trying to make me hot and bothered with promises like that."

I was happy that he was talking about coming home because for the first six months he just got quiet every time I said something about him coming home. Now, he talked about coming home and I had to do all I can to make that come true.

Since Jasmine wasn't with me, I decided to give him a show. I know he liked to see what was waiting for him at home, and besides, there were no cameras. I wore my Baby Phat jogging outfit with no panties so he can get a good view. He wasn't the only one with a good view though, because when he pulled out that fat ass dick, my mouth watered and my juices started flowing. I missed my man and felt like I was leaving a part of me behind as I left the visiting room.

I sat in the car, forcing the tears back. I got myself together before heading to the south side. It only took me fifteen minutes to get to 57th and Damen. I parked in front of the house and went up to the porch.

"Damn girl, you looking too sexy, today," Red said. "What's happening with it?"

Red was the only surviving witness in Bishop's case. I put my ear to the streets a lil while ago and tracked him down. I had been fucking with him ever since, playing him close and biding my time. I spun around so he can see the ass that I put on after having Jasmine that fit right on my body and I knew was looking damn good. These joggers were the shit. I sat down on his lap and kissed his neck.

"I just wanted to come spend some time with you and see how you doing."

"Them people just left here about an hour ago."

"Yeah? What they was talking about?"

"Same shit as before, asking questions about what happened the night I got shot and they want me to point out the nigga they got locked up for it, but I told them that I'll only talk when they take fam to trial."

"So, you gonna testify against him. That ain't what's up, baby."

I knew I was going to have to go hard to get him to change his mind but it didn't matter as long as it was for my real man.

"What you mean that ain't what's up? That nigga killed my brother, cousin and two of my homies that I grew up with. So, tell me what you think I should do."

I had to think of something fast but to stall, I asked him, "You a hood nigga, ain't you?"

"Hell, yeah, but this ain't about the streets. That shit hurt my grandma."

"I feel that but this what I'll do." I don't know where it came from but the story just rolled off my tongue. "I mean, if I was you, I'll want to body that nigga myself instead of having that nigga live, even if it's in prison."

"Damn, Toni, you a good female to have on the team. I'm going to tell the people that and handle the nigga myself."

"I'll even help you set him up when he gets out. You know a nigga can't turn this down."

I know I was putting it on thick but I had to make him believe he can get to Bishop when he got out.

"They tell you when he going to trial?"

"Even though it don't seem like it, that shit happened almost a year ago but they say in about six months. So, when you gonna let a nigga get some? You know I'm feeling you and you be teasing a nigga."

I knew that I was going to have to let him hit the pussy a few times to keep him eating out my hand and since he was going with the plan, I figured he can get a shot right now.

"I don't think you can hang with this, boy."

"Shorty, you still under yo ol' G grasp and you barely can get out to get dick, so I don't think you ready for this."

I told him I stayed with my Mom and the only way I can get out is if I sneak out when she leave or when I go to school so I didn't have to always be with him.

"Well, roll that blunt and we'll see what's up."

I ain't smoked since the time I did it to make Bishop mad but I knew I was going to need to be high for this shit.

We went into his room to smoke and all too soon the blunt was gone. He started kissing me, making me feel guilty. I started taking my clothes off so it can be over with. I climbed on the bed so he can hit it doggy style and I didn't have to see his face. I looked back at him to make sure he put the condom on. He didn't waste no time going in and after me saying a few freaky words to him, he was busting his nut.

I was so happy that it was over in two minutes and when he pulled out, he told me that it was the best pussy he ever had and that he loved me before he fell asleep. I put my clothes on and got the fuck up out of there. At home, I took a bath to wash any trace of him off of me. I was laying in the bed when Bishop called. We kicked it and I forgot all about what I did. Before the call ended, I told him to call his lawyer first thing in the morning and tell him to have the investigator go talk to the witness. The phone cut off before he could ask me anything and I went to sleep, wondering how he was going to take it when I told him what I did.

BISHOP

The punk ass lawyer keeps letting the bitch ass state play these hoe ass games with this trial date. This was the third time they wanted to push it off for another month. I hated having to sit in the bullpen every court date. It smelled like shit and piss. It's always loud and it never failed that at least two niggas got beat or stabbed up. It was like they were coming to court to get in bullshit, rather than beat their cases and go home. I was waiting on him, and as soon as my lawyer walked up to the bars of the bullpen, I went off.

"Man, what kind of bullshit is you on? I thought you said this was going to be the last time!"

"As you know, that's what the judge said but the state convinced him that they needed another month. I don't have any control over what he does. Calm down."

"Calm down! How am I suppose to calm down when I've been away from my family for eighteen months already and I gotta wait another month?!"

This dude had some nerve telling me to calm down.

"We got our shit together and I'm doing all I can to beat this case and get you back home to your family but the state is trying to keep you here. The thing is, they know their case is over so they trying to drag it out and get as many days out of you as they can. Be patient, your day will come. Believe me on that."

"I hope so, because I'm ready to go."

He left and thankfully I didn't have to wait long before they came to get us to go back to our decks. Before I got on mine, though, a CO told me I had a visit. Knowing April, she could tell I was mad and came straight here from court.

I went and sat down. I looked her in the eyes before saying, "Shorty, this shit is getting to me. These people ain't playing fair."

"It's their jobs to fuck with you baby but it's only another month and we'll be back together."

"That's the point. Last month it was another month and the same shit the month before that and the month before that. It's like they letting me see freedom, then they take it away for another month, playin' games and shit."

"Well, don't let that shit get to you. Just think what it's going to be like when you do get home."

I was finally able to smile because that was all I thought about and that's what kept me cool.

"Baby, I love you and you know when I get home, I'm going to pop triplets in you."

"Don't be making no promises that you can't keep. You know I want some more babies."

"Well, we might have to take it one at a time but they gon' look alike, so they gon' be triplets."

We got a laugh out of that and it made me forget about the extra month. I knew I was tripping anyways because dudes be in here fighting one body for three or more years and I'm fighting four bodies and an attempt but ain't been gone even two years yet.

"Baby, I got a surprise for you when you get out. You're going to like it."

"Shorty, I'm good on that party shit. Don't try that shit, again."

"Oh, we going to have a little get together with the family at the crib but it's another surprise. That's for when you get out so you'll have to wait but I got to go. Money calls. I love you, baby."

"Yeah, I love you too, Shorty."

I went back on the deck and one of the kings that I got real cool with named Looney came up to me. Looney was a small, skinny, dark-skinned Mexican with a bald head that could pass as a high school kid if he wasn't in the county jail and didn't have tattoos on his face.

"What's up, bro? What the man in the black robe say?"

"Another month. The state ain't ready again, but it ain't shit no more. I know I got this shit beat."

I really didn't like talking about getting out with him because he got caught with the smoking gun in his hand so he knew he was going to get some time. I told him that when I got out, I was going to reach back out to him and hit his books with money. I ain't tell him but I was going to see if my lawyer will take his case so he can get a good deal.

"I see your girl came straight from court."

"Yeah, you know how it is. She knew I was heated after they pulled that stunt so she had to make sure Daddy was good."

"Well, let's go to the tip and fire up this grill. I'm hungry as hell."

"Yeah, let's do that and I know that wine came off already. I need some of that."

Before I knew it, a month passed, and it was time for me to go to court again and this time we started trial.

EPILOGUE

"Mr. Tate, do you know who shot you?"

"No."

"Do you know, know of, or have you ever seen the defendant before?"

"Yeah, I know him."

I wasn't really paying attention to what was going on because I was wondering why April wasn't here for me. I knew something had to be wrong because even Mama Kelly was looking confused.

After hearing homie on the stand say he knew me I forgot about April for the time being.

"Do you know him by the name 'John Thompson' or some other name?"

I was confused when he said, "I know him by 'Bishop' but I know that his real name is, John, though."

"So, is Bishop the person that shot you, your brother, your cousin and your two childhood friends?"

"Naw, he ain't the one that did that."

His words didn't match the look he gave me and I was wondering why he was lying for me.

"But he was there that night, wasn't he?"

"Yeah, he got there a few minutes before it happened."

"Well, since he wasn't the one that shot you but he's the one that's locked up and charged for things that happened that night, can you tell us what happened that night because it's only two living victims and one is the defendant? The other is you, so can you tell us the truth."

I almost laughed, knowing that the truth will get me put under the jail.

He was quiet for a few seconds before he started.

"Okay, this what I remember before I passed out."

He paused another few seconds before he continued.

"I was kicking it with my brother when he told me that his homie Bishop was coming over. We were going to go out and get some females. My cousin and two homies was over there, too, and we were all for it, so we smoked a blunt to get in a relaxed mood."

"It was about thirty minutes before Bishop got there and he was standing by the table while we finished another blunt. We were getting ready to go when somebody came busting through the front door and started shooting. Bishop was the first one hit and he went down."

He took a drink of water, then looked around.

My lawyer jumped up. "I know this is hard and if you need a break, just let us know, okay?"

"I'm good. Like I was saying, Bishop went down. I was too shocked to move, and the next thing I know, some more people came from the back of the house and started shooting at us. I really don't know who got shot first but the last thing I remember was seeing my cousin running for the door. I blacked out then."

I turned around with a smile on my face, knowing for sure that I was going home but it went away when I realized that April still wasn't there. I didn't pay attention to the State Attorney as he tried to punch holes in dude's story or when they had closing arguments.

My mind was racing with thoughts of everything that I had to do when I got home but I tried to block it out because anything could still happen. They gave the jury the case, and me and my lawyers stayed in the court building. It took them less than thirty minutes to come back with a verdict. I re-entered the courtroom and got the surprise of a lifetime. Not only was April sitting in the front row next to Mama Kelly, but my big brother, Corn was too.

I tried to talk to him, but my lawyer kept talking to me and then the jury came in and read the verdict.

———

My homie, Looney, was waiting on me when I came back on the deck. We went in our cell before he asked, "Man, bro, what happened?"

"Man, I'm going home."

I still ain't process it yet and I wasn't going to believe it until they let me out.

"My nigga, they said not 'motha fuckin' guilty. I'm out this bitch!"

"That's what's up, bro. It good to see a good brother get out a jam."

I gave him some dap and we sat down and talked until they called me to go.

"On my mama's grave, homie you ain't got to worry about shit. I'm gon' reach for you. You're part of my family now, and I'm gonna make sure you're taken care of while you do this time."

"I know bro but get out and do the right thing. You saw what this shit is like, so avoid it at all cost."

He walked with me to the door and before leaving out, I hugged him.

It seemed like it took them forever to process me out but finally, I was free again and waiting for me was my whole family. My kids ran to me and I just held them. When I stood up, I looked from April to Corn, not knowing who to hug first but Corn helped me make up my mind.

"Nigga, she gonna be the one to give you some pussy, tonight. You better hug her first."

We all laughed and I went to give April a big hug, lifting her off the ground.

I kissed her deep and passionately. "Shorty, I love you."

"You better."

I had a million questions for Corn but all he said was, "Their C.I. got killed and that fucked up their case. Now we all home, healthy and well paid so don't worry about nothing and go have fun with yo girl."

I got in the car with April and she started telling me what she had to do to get dude to tell that story. I couldn't do nothing but thank her and even that wasn't enough.

"So, what now, boss lady?"

She been handling the business all this time, and I wasn't about to get in her way.

"Well, as of last week, the five years we agreed to with Jose and Jesus is over. We ain't got no shoebox money no more. Our shit barely fit in a safe. We can live good and leave the streets alone. What you think?"

Well, whoever said that the streets don't pay is a damn liar and despite the odds, we made it out and it wasn't by prison or a box. I don't know if my mama would've approved the way I did it but my family will be taken care of. That's all that she wanted.

THE END

ABOUT THE AUTHOR

Juhnell Morgan started writing when he was sentenced to 50 years in prison. Despite the Oddz is his first book and he is currently working on Despite the Oddz 2 and a few short stories.

Juhnell found that writing is an escape from the crazy world of prison and wants to share his gift with the world!

He would like to hear from anyone that wishes to reach out to him...

Facebook: Juhnell C. Morgan
Instagram: @juhnellmorgan

Email: juhnellmorgan@gmail.com

Or you may find his current address on his facebook page and write him directly.

OTHER BOOKS BY

Urban Aint Dead

Tales 4rm Da Dale

By **Elijah R. Freeman**

The Hottest Summer Ever

By **Elijah R. Freeman**

Hittaz 1

By **Lou Garden Price, Sr.**

The Swipe 1

By **Toola**

Street Sorority 1

By **Author Raw**

COMING SOON FROM

Urban Aint Dead

The Hottest Summer Ever 2
By **Elijah R. Freeman**

THE G-CODE
By **Elijah R. Freeman**

How To Publish A Book From Prison
By **Elijah R. Freeman**

Tales 4rm Da Dale 2
By **Elijah R. Freeman**

Hittaz 2
By **Lou Garden Price, Sr.**

The Swipe 2
By **Toola**

Street Sorority 2
By **Author Raw**

Despite The Odds 2
By **Juhnell Morgan**

Whats Done 'N The Dark
By **Diva B.**

Tales Of A Bad Chick
By **Derrick Rollins**

Cali's Cutt
By **Eliza Williams**

BOOKS BY

URBAN AINT DEAD's C.E.O

Elijah R. Freeman

Triggadale 1, 2 & 3

Tales 4rm Da Dale

The Hottest Summer Ever

Murda Was The Case 1 & 2

Follow

Elijah R. Freeman

On Social Media

FB: Elijah R. Freeman

IG: @the_future_of_urban_fiction

Made in the USA
Las Vegas, NV
13 April 2023

70532350R10177